T0197039

And yet . . . and yet, who else?

The carolers were singing. "God Rest Ye Merry Gentlemen" rang to the rafters. With a final burst of song, they retreated back into the cold Christmas Eve.

"I'm assuming your afternoon was spent rather tediously," he said, watching her expression. There was not the slightest flicker of unease in those luminous green eyes.

"If you mean ensuring that the bedchambers were allotted aright, you would be correct, sir." Lady Harriet sipped her own sherry. "Not to mention trying to keep the twins out of trouble."

Julius smiled sympathetically. She couldn't possibly have found time to comb through his bedchamber. And why would she?

She was looking utterly radiant. Her gown of bronze silk clung to her figure in a most enticing fashion. What was the matter with him? He never noticed women in any detail; he didn't have time. And a distraction could mean his life.

Not here, though, surely. He looked around the room, noting the festive air and the lively bubble of voices. What harm would it do if he indulged in a little dalliance with this alluring creature? He'd have to be blind not to appreciate her charms, and an insensate idiot not to respond to them.

But someone had been among his possessions that afternoon.

Turn the page for rave reviews of Jane Feather's wonderful stories . . .

A WEDDING WAGER

"This compelling read delivers an unforgettable cast of characters and places them in an irresistible story . . . that only an author with Feather's talents can pull off."
—*Romantic Times*

"Vivid protagonists, appealing secondary characters, and a passionate romance."
—*Publishers Weekly*

"A page turner. . . . A thoroughly enjoyable novel."
—*Romance Reviews*

RUSHED TO THE ALTAR

"Gathers momentum much like a classical opus that ends in a resounding crescendo. . . . Ms. Feather certainly knows how to titillate the imagination with some sizzling scenes set in a tapestry of bygone days."
—*Winter Haven News Chief*

"Fun and intelligent. . . . I am completely captivated."
—*Fresh Fiction*

"An ingenious story line, witty prose, and charming characters . . . a well-written addition to the historical romance genre."
—*Romance Junkies*

A HUSBAND'S WICKED WAYS

"A consummate storyteller, Feather rises to new heights in her latest Wicked novel of intrigue and desire. Her utterly engaging characters and suspenseful plot combine to hold you spellbound."
—*Romantic Times*

"Filled with recurring quirky characters, truly evil villains, and a fearless heroine who is definitely an equal to her hero."   —*Booklist*

TO WED A WICKED PRINCE

"Enchanting and witty . . . sizzling."   —*Publishers Weekly*

"A poignant love story . . . strong characters, political intrigue, secrets and passion . . . it will thrill readers and keep them turning the pages."   —*Romantic Times*

A WICKED GENTLEMAN

"Will enchant readers. . . . Filled with marvelous characters—and just enough suspense to keep the midnight oil burning."   —*Romantic Times*

"Intriguing and satisfying. . . . The captivating romance is buttressed by rich characters and an intense kidnapping subplot, making this a fine beginning for Feather's new series."   —*Publishers Weekly*

ALL THE QUEEN'S PLAYERS

"Beautifully moving . . . rich in period detail."   —*Booklist*

"A truly fantastic novel."
—*The Romance Readers Connection*

"Terrific."   —*Genre Go Round Reviews*

Also by Jane Feather

JANE FEATHER

A Holiday Novel

TWELFTH NIGHT SECRETS

POCKET BOOKS

New York   London   Toronto   Sydney   New Delhi

Pocket Books
A Division of Simon & Schuster, Inc.
1230 Avenue of the Americas
New York, NY 10020

This book is a work of fiction. Names, characters, places, and incidents either are products of the author's imagination or are used fictitiously. Any resemblance to actual events or locales or persons, living or dead, is entirely coincidental.

First Pocket Books paperback edition November 2012

POCKET and colophon are registered trademarks of
Simon & Schuster, Inc.

For information about special discounts for bulk purchases,
please contact Simon & Schuster Special Sales at 1-866-506-1949
or business@simonandschuster.com.

The Simon & Schuster Speakers Bureau can bring authors to
your live event. For more information or to book an event,
contact the Simon & Schuster Speakers Bureau at 1-866-248-3049
or visit our website at www.simonspeakers.com.

Manufactured in the United States of America

10 9 8 7 6 5 4 3 2 1

ISBN 978-1-5011-0732-0
ISBN 978-1-4391-5552-3 (ebook)

TWELFTH NIGHT SECRETS

Prologue

November 1797

Lady Harriet Devere drew her paisley wrap closer around her shoulders as a fierce wind rattled the casement behind her. Her parlor was not cold, with a blazing log fire in the grate, and it was well lit, wax candles burning brightly, but the day outside was raw, the skies heavy with gray clouds, a downpour imminent, and it did nothing to lighten her mood.

She sighed, setting down her quill, her eyes drifting to the fire. It had been many months since she had felt her customary lightheartedness, viewed the world with her usual optimism. Oh, she tried, for the children's sake, but it was hard going. Planning for the annual Christmas house party and the festivities at Charlbury had always been a joyful task, and yet this year, she could summon no enthusiasm. She turned her eyes from the fire and back to the list of names on the secretaire. The guests her grandfather had decided should be invited for this year's celebrations. So far, she had written half the invitations, and what should have taken her a couple of hours had taken all morning.

A discreet tap at the door distracted her. "Come in."

"Your pardon, my lady, but there are two gentlemen below. They would like to talk with you." The butler bowed, holding out a silver tray with two visiting cards on it.

Harriet frowned. It was not the customary hour for social visits, and she was expecting no one. She took one of the cards off the tray, and her frown deepened. *Mr. George Howard.* Just the sight of his name sent a cold shiver of apprehension down her spine. The man from the Ministry hadn't been to Grosvenor Square for ten months. Not since he'd paid a condolence visit on the death of her brother. She looked at the other card. The name, *Mr. Anthony Bedford,* was unknown to her.

"Show them into the yellow salon, Dickson. I'll be down in a few minutes." After the butler had withdrawn, she sat at the secretaire in frowning thought for a while. *What could Howard want? The work is over now . . . it has been almost a year since the last letter from Nick.*

Well, Harriet thought, she wouldn't find out by speculating. She set aside her quill and rose from the desk, checking her reflection automatically in the mirror above the pier table. She was still in half mourning, and her gown of dove gray seemed to leach the color from her complexion, dulling the golden sheen in the braided coronet of her hair. It was time to leave mourning behind her. The Duke of Charlbury had instructed his granddaughter in no uncertain terms that Christmas would not be overshadowed by past sorrows. It was time to look forward and embrace the world again. Nicholas would have wanted it. And in truth, Harriet reflected, Nick *would* have wanted it. He detested gloom and low spirits.

She hurried downstairs. A footman opened the door to the yellow drawing room for her. It was a more informal room than the main salon at the front of the house, and Harriet used it almost exclusively when it was only she and the twins in residence in town.

The two men standing in front of the fire turned as one to greet her as she quietly closed the door behind her. "Lady Harriet, thank you for seeing us without notice," Mr. Howard said with a bow. "Allow me to present my colleague, Anthony Bedford."

"Mr. Howard . . . Mr. Bedford, it's a pleasure." She acknowledged their bows with the slightest curtsy. "Pray sit down. May I offer you some refreshment?"

"No, thank you, Lady Harriet." It was Mr. Bedford who spoke, and Harriet noticed that his companion stepped back slightly, as if to exclude himself from the conversation. Bedford was at first glance so unassuming as to be almost invisible. A gray man from top to toe, short gray hair, dark gray woolen coat and britches, even his deep-set eyes were gray, but the overall dullness of his appearance was enlivened by those eyes, which had a deep and penetrating gleam that Harriet felt was seeing into her very thoughts.

She offered a bland smile and invited them again to sit down. Howard did so, but his companion remained standing with his back to the fire.

Harriet debated whether to sit down herself or whether that would put her at a disadvantage. For some reason, she felt certain that in this man's company, she did not want to be at any disadvantage. She compromised and perched on the arm of a sofa. "To what do I owe the pleasure, gentlemen?"

"We will come straight to the point, ma'am," Bedford replied.

"Please do, sir." Harriet inclined her head with the appearance of cool composure.

"You are familiar with the work your brother, Viscount Hesketh, was doing for the Ministry of War," he stated. "Indeed, you have been of some service to the Ministry yourself in the past."

"A very minor role, Mr. Bedford," Harriet said. "I merely received my brother's correspondence from Europe and passed it on to Mr. Howard. I would hardly say I was of much importance."

"You do yourself a disservice, Lady Harriet," he said drily. "Without people like you, our part of the war effort could not be performed. However, we have another task for you, if you would be willing to undertake it . . . a rather more significant mission."

Harriet shot an involuntary glance towards the man she knew from the past. George Howard offered her a fleeting smile that if it was meant to reassure her didn't really do the job. "Pray continue," she said to Bedford.

"Your brother's death—"

"At the siege of Elba," she interrupted with a touch of impatience.

"Lord Hesketh did not die on the battlefield as you supposed, ma'am. He was assassinated while on a clandestine mission for us."

"But . . . but it said in the *Gazette,* the letter from the Ministry said, Nick died in the siege."

"Sometimes, Lady Harriet, we do not always tell the exact truth where work for the clandestine branch of the Ministry is concerned. I'm sure you understand why." His tone was as dry as before.

She nodded. "Yes, I'm sure that's so." It was obvious, of course. It was inevitable that a man who lived in those shadows would die in them eventually. It made no difference to the essential fact. Nick was gone. It didn't really matter how his death had come about.

"We would like to discover who killed your brother, Lady Harriet."

Harriet frowned. "And I can help you do that?"

"You can help us investigate one possibility," George Howard chipped in.

She felt a strange little tingle of . . . of what? Anticipation? Apprehension? *Excitement*? Surely not. "I don't understand."

"Allow me to explain, ma'am." Bedford spoke again and continued as if he were reading from a list in a catalogue. "One of your brother's colleagues was in the area when your brother was murdered. Indeed, they had been working partners for quite some time. This man, during his friendship with Lord Hesketh, became a welcome visitor at your grandfather's house, Charlbury Hall. The Duke has welcomed him there on several occasions since Lord Hesketh's death. We would like to know whether this man is playing to a different drummer . . . a double agent, in other words. We know there is a nest of French spies embedded at the university at Oxford, a mere ten miles from Charlbury. Julius Forsythe, the Earl of Marbury, has been invited by your grandfather to Charlbury Hall for Christmas. Since you will also be there, in a particularly convenient position as hostess, we would ask you to watch the Earl, see where he goes, listen to what he says, see if he sends correspondence out of the house. Just general observation . . . nothing more elaborate than that, and there should be no danger at all as long as you don't exceed your remit."

"This Julius Forsythe . . . Lord Marbury . . . is the man who was Nick's partner?" Harriet felt the need to clarify every detail, however stupid she might sound.

"That is so, Lady Harriet. He may not have been responsible for your brother's death—indeed, he may well not be a double agent—but we would like to know a little more about his present activities."

"I was under the impression that your spies worked under close supervision," Harriet said, a touch of acid in her tone. She felt ambushed in some way, and she felt very much at a disadvantage.

"The good ones tend to run themselves, ma'am." That arid tone again, but this time it was accompanied by just the tiniest twitch of thin lips. "Julius Forsythe is one of the best."

"If not *the* best," added George Howard.

"If not *the* best," his colleague agreed.

Harriet rose from her perch and crossed to the window that looked out over the small walled garden, November-bare now, but the camellia bushes against the red wall were just coming into flower. This man was going to be at Charlbury for Christmas, whether she liked it or not. She could not countermand her grandfather's invitation. And if he had killed Nick . . . a slow rage began to burn deep in her belly. It was one thing to imagine her brother killed by an unknown assailant on a battlefield, quite another to think of him stabbed in the back by someone he knew. A friend . . . a partner.

She spun back to the salon and the two men,

watching her in silence. "Very well. I will do what I can."

"You will have your country's gratitude, my lady." George Howard bowed deeply. "And you will help to avenge a grave wrong done to one of our own."

"Indeed, ma'am." Anthony Bedford took up his gloves, discarded on a small table. "Maybe it will help you in your mission to know that your father, too, served his country in this way. He, too, died from an assassin's blade. Your brother was following in his father's footsteps."

"A family business, then." Harriet's lips twisted into a wry smile. Somehow this didn't come as that much of a surprise. After everything else, it seemed logical that she should simply take up the mantle and do her part.

And avenge her brother into the bargain.

Chapter One

"Harry . . . Harry, you're not asleep, your eyes are open, but you're not listening to us."

Lady Harriet Devere jerked herself out of her reverie and devoted her attention to her young siblings. "Forgive me, you're right. I was miles away. What was it you were saying?"

"How much longer?" the twins, as they did so often, chorused in unison. "We're tired of traveling."

"I don't blame you, so am I," their sister said with a rueful smile. They had been traveling since dawn that morning. She glanced at her fob watch. It was almost four o'clock, and the December light beyond the carriage window was gray with the beginnings of dusk. She opened the window, letting in a blast of frigid air, and called up to the coachman.

"Carson, where are we now?"

"Just past Woodstock, Lady Harriet. Another half hour should do it, I reckon," he called down.

Harriet withdrew her head and closed the window. The glass panes were a luxury, but the Devere family was well able to afford such amenities. "Not long now, then," she said cheerfully. "Now, don't forget not to shout around Grandfather. I know it's Christmas, and it's exciting, but you know how he hates raised voices, and you don't wish to get on his bad side. He can make life rather unpleasant."

"Oh, we know." The pair groaned, rolling their green eyes.

"Last time we were at Charlbury," Lady Grace said, "he wouldn't let us ride our ponies for a week because we were playing a game in the hall and knocked over the crystal vase on the pier table."

Harriet smiled to herself. Lionel Devere, Duke of Charlbury, was a formidable gentleman, but he had a soft spot for his grandchildren, except on the occasions when their rambunctious play intruded on his scholarly pursuits. He could be particularly hard on Tom, now his heir after the deaths of Lionel's eldest son, Edward, and then his grandson, Nicholas. The Duke maintained that Tom had to be held to a higher standard than most ten-year-old boys if he was to assume the ducal mantle one day.

Harriet's smile faded. How she missed her brother. The pain of her father's loss had diminished over time, but it was still there, a distant ache. Both of them lost to an assassin's knife.

And now here she was, dipping her toes into the same devious world that had swallowed her father and her brother. An inner compulsion drove her, had done so from the first moment the man from the Ministry had recruited her into that world. Helping to avenge the family deaths gave her a sense of purpose that had been missing since her brother's death and seemed to soften the edges of her ever-present grief.

What would he be like, this Julius Forsythe, Earl of Marbury? He had known her brother, which should have spoken well for him, but if he was what the Ministry suspected, then he was lower than a maggot. For a moment, she indulged her anger, imagining how her own actions would squash the maggot underfoot. But then she reminded herself that hers was an investigative mission. The man had not yet been proven guilty; her task was to find the proof if it existed. It would be up to her masters in Horseguards Parade to decide what to do with the traitor, if that was what the Earl turned out to be.

The Earl of Marbury was at this point aiming his gun at a skein of geese flying low in the dusk over the lake on the Devere estate. One bird, gallantly bringing up the rear at the long-drawn-out tail of its fellows, was falling behind, a perfectly isolated target for his lordship's weapon. The Earl sighted, his finger resting on the trigger, but when he was certain the shot would have been a good one, bringing his quarry down onto the smooth waters of the lake, he lowered his gun. The pleasure was in the skill of a successful shot, not in the death of a creature that would probably not be good eating, anyway . . . too scrawny with the effort of keeping up with its peers. The young retriever panting at his heels looked up at him with an air of surprise and a certain resentment at having been deprived of her swim to retrieve a fallen bird.

Julius patted the dog's head. "Never mind, Tess, another day. One bird wouldn't feed the Christmas table here, anyway." He broke open his gun and unloaded it, before tucking it into the crook of his elbow and heading back through the lightly wooded copse around the lake towards the brilliantly lit gray stone pile of Charlbury Hall. The grass scrunched under his boots as the evening frost formed, and a cold wind knifed through his jacket, carrying the smell of snow.

Charlbury Hall, which dominated the surrounding landscape from a small rise, was a glowing oasis floating in the gathering darkness. Lamplight shone in every window on the first three floors; only the servants' attics were in darkness. The golden light flooded the neat green lawns, sweeping from the house to the lake, and illuminated the circular driveway in front of the great double doors.

Those doors stood open now, and a carriage was drawn up before them. Footmen, shouldering portmanteaux and trunks, hurried up the shallow flight of stairs into the bright hall. Julius paused on the edge of the lawn, Tess at his heels, watching. He recognized the Devere arms on the panels of the carriage.

So, Nicholas's sister had arrived. He felt a quickening of interest. Nick had talked much of his sister, Lady Harriet, or Harry, as she was called by her siblings. He had painted a picture of a paragon of wit and beauty, and Julius was curious to see how much of that praise was a result of brotherly bias.

A pair of small figures sprang from the coach, darted between the servants unloading the vehicle, and scampered towards the side of the house. A clear voice called, "Tom, Gracie, where are you going?"

"To see Judd," childish voices chorused, carrying easily through the crisp, frosty December air.

"Back soon . . ." one of them added, as if in reassurance, and the figures disappeared around the building.

The first voice belonged to a woman standing on the bottom step of the house. She wore a dark traveling cloak, the fur-edged hood pulled up so Julius could get no impression of her appearance. She shook her head as if in mild exasperation and continued up the stairs into the house. Julius turned to a side path that would take him into the house through the gun room. He would make the acquaintance of Lady Harriet Devere soon enough.

Harriet entered the family home with a sense of comfort that its familiarity always engendered. For one who had not been brought up amidst its splendors, it could well prove intimidating, but she had been born in one of the grand bedrooms and spent her childhood in the nurseries on the third floor. She had had her own bedroom on the adult floor since her fourteenth birthday, and from the day she had put up her hair and had had her debutante Season, she had played hostess for her grandfather. There was nothing on this ducal estate that was unfamiliar.

"Harriet, my dear. You made good time." The Duke of Charlbury came across the expanse of marble floor to greet her with hands outstretched. He was a big man, broad-shouldered, with the upright posture and weather-beaten complexion of a sportsman. But Harriet thought he looked a little tired, his green eyes a little more faded than when she'd last seen him, and she thought she could begin to detect just the slightest stoop to those broad shoulders. Grief had most assuredly taken its toll, but the stoop also had something to do with the hours the old man spent secluded in his library, poring over the scholarly tomes that gave him so much intellectual pleasure. Nevertheless, despite these signs of aging, it was still hard to believe that Lionel was close to the end of his eighth decade.

"Grandfather." She took his hands, then hugged him fiercely, kissing his cheek. "The journey was good, and the children were as patient as one could ever expect them to be."

"And where are those hellions?" The Duke looked around with raised eyebrows.

"Oh, they ran off to see Judd in the stables as soon as we arrived." Harriet drew off her gloves.

"Well, that should give me no illusions about a grandfather's place in their priorities," Lionel said drily.

"Now, don't be severe, sir," Harriet responded, smiling. "They've been cooped up since dawn. It's much better if they run off the fidgets now."

He gave a mock sigh. "I suppose you're right. This house has stood through invasion, civil war, and God only knows what other upheavals, but nothing comes near to those brats when it comes to the power of destruction."

Harriet was about to protest when she caught a flicker in her peripheral vision and turned her head sharply to the shadows at the rear of the hall where a passage entered from the gun room. Her grandfather followed her gaze, and a smile touched his finely sculpted mouth. "Ah, Marbury, my dear fellow, come and meet my granddaughter. Harriet, this is Lord Marbury . . . sir, Lady Harriet Devere."

Julius stepped into the light, the retriever clinging to his heels. "An honor, ma'am. Please forgive my country attire. I was on my way to change my dress." He no longer carried his gun, but his boots were muddied, and his plain woolen britches and jacket were cut comfortably for sporting pursuits. His bow, however, would have been perfectly appropriate for a Queen's Drawing Room, and there was a pleasant easiness about his manner that she warmed to instantly.

And just as instantly she reminded herself that this was her quarry. A suspected traitor, the man who it was believed had betrayed her brother. But Julius Forsythe didn't know anyone suspected that, and he mustn't. Any more than he must ever suspect her own mission at Charlbury Hall this Christmas.

Her smile was all affability as she curtsied, saying, "Indeed, sir, think nothing of it. We are in the country, after all." She bent smiling to the dog, extending her flat palm so the retriever could take her scent. "And who is this pretty lady?"

"Tess, ma'am. She's young yet but is training well." He laid a hand on the dog's head, and Tess lifted her head against his palm.

Harriet straightened. "If you'll excuse me, I must see to the unpacking and sort out the children." She turned to the butler, who stood attentively at the foot of the stairs. "Mallow, would you send to the stables for Lady Grace and Lord Hesketh? I need them in the nursery." It always felt strange to give Tom the courtesy title he had inherited from his brother, but now that Nicholas was dead, Tom was the heir to the dukedom. He would presumably grow into the role, she thought, firmly squashing any doubts on the subject with the reflection that it was very early days yet.

"Right away, my lady." The butler moved off in stately fashion, beckoning to a liveried footman.

"I'll see them in the library when they're respectable," the Duke declared. "Bring them to me there, Harriet . . . oh, and they may as well dine downstairs, as we're to be informal tonight."

Harriet curtsied her acknowledgment, and her grandfather returned to his library.

Lord Marbury stood aside so that she could precede him up the stairs. "How was the journey from London?"

"Tedious, but no worse than that," she responded with what she hoped was a cool smile. "I gather your retriever does not sleep in the kennels with the other dogs."

"No. They have a tendency to bully her, and I'll not have her spirit broken," he stated, following her up. "When she's old enough to hold her own, then time enough."

A somewhat sentimental attitude to a sporting dog, Harriet thought, but one she could only applaud. It seemed strangely sensitive, though, in one who was as ruthless as he was said to be.

They parted company on the galleried landing above the great hall, Harriet going towards her own apartments at the front of the house, his lordship taking the left wing to the guest apartments. The double doors to Harriet's bedchamber and boudoir stood open. Lamplight filled the spacious chamber, and a bright log fire burned in the grate. A very young maidservant, in the midst of unpacking her ladyship's trunk, turned as Harriet entered and curtsied. "Good evening, m'lady."

"Good evening." Harriet smiled pleasantly, closing the double doors behind her. "How warm and welcoming it is in here." She raised an interrogative eyebrow. "You're new to Charlbury, aren't you?" She unclasped her cloak.

"Yes, m'lady. Agnes, at your service, ma'am. My ma's been 'ead parlor maid for five years, and I was took on in the scullery first. This is my first job abovestairs. I'm to be your lady's maid, and I 'ope to give satisfaction, m'lady." She looked anxiously at Harriet as she curtsied again. "I'm a dab 'and with the flat iron, ma'am, and even Ma says as 'ow I'm a first-rate seamstress."

"I'm sure we shall deal very well together, Agnes," Harriet responded with a friendly smile, guessing that her own reputation for being an easy and undemanding mistress had influenced the housekeeper's decision to place this child with her for her first essay into the rarefied world of ladies' maids. "Would you ring for some tea?" She cast her cloak over the back of an armless chair and went to warm her hands at the fire.

Agnes pulled vigorously on the bell rope beside the fireplace and picked up the discarded cloak, hurrying to hang it in the armoire. "What gown will you wear this evenin', m'lady? I'll take it to the laundry room for a touch-up before you dress. Everything's a bit creased from the trunk." She gestured to the scattered piles of richly colored silks, muslins, and velvets spread out upon the bed.

Harriet looked them over. The guests for the annual Christmas house party would not be arriving until tomorrow. She had arrived a day early to ensure that all the arrangements were in hand for their reception and the entertainments to follow. Her grandfather, of course, would take care of the gentlemen's pursuits and would already have arranged with his steward and gamekeepers for hunting and shooting parties, but many of the ladies required a succession of less energetic enjoyments. And, of course, there was food. The constant supply of delicacies, both solid and liquid, was essential to the success of a house party.

But for this evening, the family would dine alone and informally. Except, of course, for the guest who was already there. Harriet frowned. Her grandfather's guest list had included the Earl, but he had said nothing to her about inviting him ahead of time. Bedford had told her that Marbury would be a member of the house party but, again, had failed to mention his premature arrival. It seemed to imply a friendship between the Duke and the Earl that went beyond their shared connection to Nick and despite a considerable age difference. And Lionel wanted the children to join them at dinner, which was unheard of except in a very intimate family setting. So how long had he felt so close to Julius Forsythe? And why, if they were old friends, had his name never come up in conversation? Nicholas hadn't mentioned him to his sister, either, but she had assumed from what she had been told by Bedford that their acquaintance was new and confined only to the clandestine work they shared. It seemed this was yet another conundrum in the strange world she had entered, where nothing was as it seemed.

Her hand hovered over a simple lavender silk day gown that would be entirely suitable for an intimate family dinner. But they weren't to be just family, were they? Maybe, bearing in mind their guest, she should make a little more effort . . . she was supposed to cultivate the Earl, after all.

"I'll wear this, Agnes." She selected an evening gown of rose-pink taffeta, the décolleté neckline and tiny puffed sleeves embroidered with seed pearls. She would compromise by wearing only a simple strand of pearls and dressing her hair in a plain knot on her nape with just a few side curls. "Ah, tea . . . thank you." She turned as a maidservant brought in a tray of tea. "Just set it by the fire, please."

"I'll press the gown now, then, shall I, m'lady . . . or should I finish unpacking first?" Agnes looked in indecision between the gown and the armoire.

"Finish unpacking first," Harriet instructed. "Dinner will not be for another two hours, but I should like a bath beforehand. It's been a long day of traveling." She poured tea.

"Oh, yes, right away, m'lady." Agnes started for the door and then stopped. "Oh, but should I unpack first?"

"Ring the bell for water, sheets for the floor, and the hip bath, Agnes, and you may safely leave the footmen to bring those up while you finish unpacking." Harriet was aware that she could have instructed the footmen herself, but she also knew that Agnes's fragile standing as lady's maid would be severely damaged belowstairs if she did so.

"Yes, m'lady." With obvious relief, Agnes pulled the bell and then turned back to the unpacking.

Harriet sipped her tea and then set down the cup at the sound of feet pounding on the stairs and racing down the gallery before her door flew open. "Oh, Harry, there's a new colt. Judd says he's out of Sultana by Atlas . . . he's beautiful. You have to come and see him." The twins hurled themselves into the room, their words bursting out before them.

"Tomorrow I shall," their sister said calmly, taking up her cup again. They were looking singularly untidy, and Tom seemed to have acquired half a hay bale in his unruly strawberry-blond curls. "Come, you need to go to Nurse Maddox, she'll be waiting for you. You're to dine downstairs tonight with the Duke, and if he sees you looking like that, he'll banish you to the nursery until the New Year." She finished her tea and rose to her feet. "I'll have my bath when I get back, Agnes." Sweeping the children in front of her as if she were a broom, she hustled them out and towards the nursery stairs at the rear of the house, their excited chatter continuing unabated.

Nurse Maddox, the formidable ruler of the nurseries through two generations of Deveres, was instructing two assistant nursemaids in the unpacking and disposal of the children's belongings. She lived a life of peaceful retirement except when the twins were in residence, at which point she energetically assumed the nursery reins, ruling her small empire with the proverbial iron fist and velvet glove. The twins adored her, for all that they held her in awed respect, as, indeed, did their older siblings.

She turned as the children burst into the day nursery, still extolling the virtues of the new colt. "Ah, so that's where you've been," she declared, untangling the narrative threads with experienced ease. "I might have known." She plucked a straw from Tom's hair before turning her attention to their elder sister, examining her closely. "Lady Harriet, you look fatigued."

"Just the journey, Nurse," Harriet responded cheerfully. "I shall be right as rain after a bath."

"Dinner and an early night is what you need." The woman nodded to punctuate the statement and surveyed the twins. "What a pair of rapscallions you are. You both look as if you've been dragged through a hedge backwards."

"Well, not exactly," Grace said. "It wasn't a hedge exactly."

"No, it was the hayloft," Tom supplied. "We went up there to get some oats for the colt."

"Judd said we could," his sister chimed in with a self-righteous air.

"Be that as it may, you both need to wash and change before you visit your grandfather," Harriet said swiftly. "The Duke wishes them to dine below tonight, Nurse."

Nurse received the information with a disapproving sniff, but she would never utter a word of criticism of her employer. "We'd best be getting on, then. Lord knows how long it'll take to get them respectable."

Harriet made her escape, leaving her now relatively subdued siblings to the efficient attentions of

Nurse Maddox, and hurried to her own chamber to luxuriate in the waiting bath. She must pay a visit to the kitchen before dinner and another to the butler's pantry and the housekeeper's sitting room to offer her customary speech of appreciation for all the work they had done and would be doing over the next twelve days. The Duke's steward would have arranged for the Christmas boxes, which would be presented to the staff on Boxing Day, the day after Christmas, when they would have their own holiday between breakfast and dinner. Most of the house party would be out on the Boxing Day hunt and would fend for themselves in the local hostelries at midday. Those who remained at Charlbury Hall would make do with a cold collation. She must remember to check with Cook that there was a plentiful supply of partridge pies . . .

Harriet's eyelids drooped as the steam rose from the hip bath, and for a moment she slipped into a trancelike doze, still feeling the rocking of the carriage over the rutted roads. She jerked awake when Agnes coughed vigorously from the far side of the screen.

"Ma'am, 'tis past six o'clock. Will you get dressed now?"

"Oh, Lord, is it that late?" Harriet heaved herself

inelegantly from the tub, heedless of the slurp of soapy water over the edge and onto the thickly piled sheets. She took the towel that had been warming over the top of the screen and wrapped herself tightly before emerging into the chamber. "We need to be quick, Agnes. Do you have any skill at dressing hair?"

"I can do the simple styles, ma'am." Agnes held out the thin silk chemise.

Harriet slipped it over her head and sat down to draw on the silk stockings, fastening them above the knee with silk ribbon garters. She stood to allow Agnes to drop the delicate taffeta gown over her head and adjust the dramatic black velvet belt just under her breasts, which swelled over the neckline of a bodice that was little more than four inches deep. It was a flimsy garment to wear in a huge and drafty country house in midwinter, but when fashion dictates, a lady must obey, she thought wryly, draping a black cashmere shawl over her arms. She sat down at the dresser mirror, unpinning her hair from the knot that had kept it dry in the bath.

"Could you brush it for me, please, Agnes, then we'll gather it into a coil on my neck and just tease out a few side ringlets."

She opened her jewel casket as the girl brushed the

pale gold hair where just the faintest hints of straw-
berry red caught the lamplight. The pearl choker nestled close to her throat and quickly took on the warm
glow from her skin. She clasped a matching bracelet
at her wrist and nodded her satisfaction as Agnes put
the last pin in the coil on her nape.

"Very nice, Agnes. Thank you." The girl blushed
with pleasure.

A vigorous knocking at the door and a chorus of
"Harry, can we come in, Harry?" heralded the arrival
of the children, who entered without waiting for permission. "We look very tidy," Grace declared. "Nurse
said so."

"She was right," their sister concurred, rising from
the dresser stool. "That's a very pretty gown, Gracie."
She was pleased to see that her little sister seemed
to like the compliment, smoothing down her white
muslin skirts with a little, almost feminine gesture.
Lady Grace in general bore little resemblance to her
name, preferring to scramble with her brother up hill
and down dale to the pursuits considered suitable for
a young girl. Harriet didn't blame her in the least;
she herself had been the despair of her parents in her
childhood, reveling in the tomboy activities of her
brother, only a year older than herself. They, too,

had grown up almost as twins. Irish twins, Nurse had called them.

"I look smart, too, don't I?" Tom asked with a quick frown. His nankeen britches, white frilled shirt, and short jacket were, for the moment, pristine, and his hair had been brushed ruthlessly into something approaching neatness.

"Indeed, you do, Tom. Let us go and present you to the Duke." She ushered them from the chamber and down the grand curving sweep of the horseshoe staircase, holding them firmly by the hand in case it occurred to one of them to take the time-honored route down the shiny banister rail. She knocked on the library door and at the Duke's bidding swept the children ahead of her into the large paneled salon.

"Here are the children, sir."

Lionel was taking his ease in a large winged chair in front of the fire, a glass of sherry in hand, a book on his knee. He looked up and regarded his youngest grandchildren with a barely concealed twinkle in his eye. Privately, he relished their spirit and independence, knowing it was a Devere quality that should never be repressed, but he rarely permitted them to see his indulgence. His older grandchildren, Nick and Harriet, had learned this indulgence only when they had showed sufficient maturity to accept it without taking advantage of it, and the Duke had every intention that these two youngest offspring of his beloved son would follow the same path.

"Come here, let me look at you." He beckoned them over.

They approached cautiously. Grace, at a slight nudge from her elder sister, curtsied with a murmured "Good evening, sir," and Tom produced a jerky bow and a similar greeting.

"You have things to do, Harriet," the Duke declared, glancing at his elder granddaughter. "Go and do what you must. The children and I will renew our acquaintance."

"Thank you, sir." Harriet dropped her own curtsy and abandoned her siblings with barely a flicker of anxiety. They would relax quickly enough, and once they were themselves, they were, as she knew, irresistible, even to the Duke of Charlbury.

She hesitated in the hall, wondering which of her housekeeping tasks she could accomplish first, and then, on impulse, headed for the stairs. It behooved her to ensure that their guest had everything he required.

Chapter Two

Harriet turned to the guest wing at the top of the staircase and walked down the wide corridor. Most of the doors stood open, beds made, small fires in the grates to air the rooms before their occupants arrived the next day. A footman emerged from a coveted corner bedchamber at the end of the corridor. She paused, waiting for him to reach her.

"Are you waiting upon the Earl, Thomas?"

"Yes, m'lady. He left his own man behind in London."

"And is everything going smoothly?"

"Oh, yes, m'lady. His lordship's very pleasant to work for. His wardrobe's in the front of fashion; it's a pleasure to assist with his dress." The footman was smiling broadly, and Harriet guessed he had received a douceur in advance from his gentleman, always a wise move when one was relying on strange servants to assist with one's personal needs.

"Good." She gave him a pleasant nod. "If there are problems, you'll discuss them with Mrs. Sutcliff or Mr. Mallow."

"Of course, ma'am. But I don't anticipate any." He bowed and hurried away.

Harriet continued down the corridor. The door to the corner chamber was ajar, lamplight throwing a narrow beam into the corridor. She paused, her hand raised to tap upon the door, but something made her hesitate. The Earl's figure appeared in the gap, bending over a lit candle. He held a piece of paper in his hand, his eyes upon it, then touched the edge to the candle flame. The parchment caught fire, and he held it steady until it was down to the far corner, then let the ashes fall to the table. Swiftly, he swept up the gray heap into the palm of his hand and turned to drop the ashes into the fire.

Now, why didn't he simply burn the paper in the fire in the first place? Harriet wondered, until it occurred to her that sometimes odd scraps drifted to the back of the hearth and could be retrieved when the grate was swept.

Maybe the Earl was overcautious, but if what he had burned was for his eyes only, then he had his reasons.

Dear heaven, she was thinking like a spy herself now—amazing how quickly one caught on. It was a sardonic reflection, and she was about to turn away, suddenly feeling uncomfortably like a voyeur, when the door was abruptly pulled wide open, and the Earl stood there, regarding her through a quizzing glass. His thick dark hair was cut in the new shorter style, brushed back from a broad, intelligent brow. His plain white cravat was tied high under his throat, a diamond pin throwing blue fire in its folds. His cutaway black wool coat and close-fitting knee britches set off his tall, slender figure to perfection. She absorbed all of this inadvertently despite her shock and embarrassment.

His black eyes held a glimmer of knowing amusement that added to her discomfort. "Ah," he said. "I had a feeling someone was hovering. Is there something I can do for you, Lady Harriet? Or is your visit purely coincidental?" There was a slightly mocking tone to his rich voice that made her hackles rise and deepened her sense of chagrin. She felt like a small child caught stealing cake. She managed what she hoped was a collected, noncommittal smile.

"Neither, my lord. I merely wished to be sure that everything was in order and you were quite satisfied with Thomas."

"Perfectly, thank you."

He stepped into the corridor, closing the door firmly at his back. "Are you going downstairs? May I escort you?"

"I have some housekeeping visits to make first," she responded with a slight curtsy. "The Duke is in the library. I should warn you that he has my twin siblings with him. I'm sure in their grandfather's presence, they're well under control, but they can be a little volatile on occasion."

"Nothing that will surprise me, I'm certain, Lady Harriet. My sister has a large brood, so I'm quite accustomed to the company of small fry. Indeed, I enjoy it." He bowed over her hand. "I will see you shortly."

She smiled her acknowledgment, and he strolled off down the corridor to the galleried landing without a backwards glance.

Harriet pursed her lips, watching him walk away. It seemed incongruous that such a man should confess to enjoying the company of children, as out of place as his solicitude for his young dog. But then, the face of villainy had many expressions. She waited until he turned the corner to the landing, then laid her hand firmly on the door latch, lifting it slowly. She had every right to enter the guest chambers in her role as hostess, so why was her heart beating so fast as she pushed open the door onto the warmly lit room? Tess, curled up on a blanket in front of the fire, raised her head incuriously as she stepped inside.

"It's all right, Tess. It's only me," Harriet murmured, and with a breathy sigh, the dog rested her head on her paws again, but her brown eyes were alert, watching the visitor's every move.

Well, at least dogs don't tell tales, Harriet reflected as her eye swept the chamber. She could see nothing out of place. What was she looking for, anyway? Why did she imagine that this accomplished spy would leave anything incriminating available to prying eyes?

A neat stack of papers lay on the secretaire in the window embrasure, and she walked over to the desk. If anyone wanted to know why she was there, she was merely ensuring that their guest had a plentiful supply of ink and quills. She was fairly certain such an explanation would not satisfy the black-eyed Earl of Marbury, and her heart beat even faster as she glanced anxiously over her shoulder towards the door, which she had left ajar, thinking it would look less incriminating if she had an unexpected visitor.

A sheet of vellum bore the imprint of a quill as if it had been beneath a paper he had been writing on. She squinted at the marks, unwilling to pick up the paper in case she disturbed something that would indicate interference with his possessions. She could make out little from the deep indentations; they seemed to be meaningless, random letters and numbers. Although presumably, they made sense to their intended recipient. Was it a response to the letter he had just burned?

Tess began to get to her feet, and Harriet decided she had done enough prying for one day. She dropped a reassuring hand onto the dog's head, before hurrying with relief from the room, closing the door softly behind her with the reflection that spying didn't seem to come naturally to her, despite the fact that the aptitude appeared to be a family trait.

Downstairs, she made her way to the housekeeper's parlor. Mrs. Sutcliff was examining a sheaf of accounts when Harriet tapped lightly at her open door. "Mrs. Sutcliff, I'm sorry to disturb you."

"Not at all, my lady." The housekeeper rose to her feet with a curtsy. Now in middle life, she had been in service at Charlbury Hall since her eleventh birthday and was convinced that the house would fall apart if she was not controlling every aspect of its running. Grudgingly, she allowed Mallow, the butler, to control his own realm, and Harriet was always careful to grant her all due respect, steering her own delicate path through the rivalry between Mallow and the housekeeper.

"Oh, do sit down, Mrs. Sutcliff. I know you're busy, but I just wished to see if there were any questions I could answer about the guests or anything I should know about with the staff. Is all well?"

"Aye, well enough, m'lady." The housekeeper sat down again. "Young Doris has the toothache, and we may have to do without her for a day or two. She needs the tooth pulled, but she'll have to be dragged to the dentist, I fear. It'll wait until after Christmas, mind. When she's suffered for a few more days, she may be a bit more willing." The woman gave a nod of severe satisfaction.

Harriet grimaced. Toothache was the very devil, and she could sympathize with poor little Doris. The scullery maid was no more than a child. "Well, if we have oil of cloves in the still room, Mrs. Sutcliff, that might relieve her pain a little."

"That's been taken care of, ma'am," the woman responded with a little sniff. "And her jaw's bound tight in flannel."

"Yes, of course," Harriet said hastily. "Of course you would know exactly what to do for the girl. Is there anything else?"

"No, m'lady, nothing I can think of," the house-keeper said, mollified. "But you may be sure now you've arrived, you'll be informed, and I'll do myself the honor of waiting upon you with Cook's menus after breakfast."

"Thank you." Harriet smiled and took herself off to the butler's pantry. These few minutes with the senior staff whenever she arrived paid off, she knew, but she found them a sore trial.

A few appreciative words for Mallow, who was cleaning the vast array of family silver, a task he held dear, followed by a visit to the steaming, insanely hectic kitchen, where pots and cauldrons bubbled on the range and a pot boy sat turning a suckling pig on a spit over the open fire, and she considered her duty done. She stepped back into the expanse of the hall, cool despite the massive yule log burning in a fireplace big enough to roast an ox, and took a moment to examine her reflection in the gilt-framed mirror beside the door. Her cheeks were a little flushed from the heat in the kitchen, but other than that, everything seemed to be in order. She went to the library, nodding her thanks to the footman, who hurried to open the double doors for her.

"Ah, there you are, Harriet. Everything running smoothly in our little realm?" Lionel greeted her with a smile. The Earl rose to his feet and bowed. The children, sitting side-by-side on an ottoman at their grandfather's feet, burst into speech before she had time to respond to the Duke.

"Grandfather says we can join the Boxing Day hunt, Harry. Only we have to have Judd with us, and he'll bring us back at lunchtime. Grandfather says we're not old enough to stay out all day, but we are, aren't we, Harry?"

"Sherry, Lady Harriet, or Madeira? You may need fortification before you answer." The Earl had moved to the decanters on the sideboard. He was smiling, and his eyes looked quite different. Instead of the mocking gleam she had seen before, the glint of amusement seemed purely one of enjoyment, and there was a sparkle to their dark depths that she warmed to despite herself.

"Sherry, thank you." She sat down on a sofa, thinking that the Earl seemed to be very much at home, dispensing his host's hospitality as easily as her brother would have done. She glanced at her grandfather, who showed no signs of annoyance at this presumption, instead holding out his own glass for a refill.

"We can, can't we, Harry?" Tom prompted, bringing her back to the matter in hand.

"If the Duke says you may go out for half a day, then you may go out for half a day," Harriet stated, taking her sherry from the Earl with a polite nod of acknowledgment. "You will be sufficiently fatigued by lunchtime to be glad to come home to a hot bath, I promise you."

"*Harry,*" they chorused, their expressions showing mingled disbelief and shock at their sister's betrayal.

She laughed at their indignation, aware of the Earl's open amusement. "You'll see, I promise you."

"Nick would've let us," Grace said, her voice rather small.

"Yes," her brother chimed in. "Nick would have let us ride with him."

"If you'll accept me as a substitute for your brother, I will undertake to ensure that you miss none of the excitement in the morning." Julius bent down a little to the twins. "If you stay with me for the first hour, we'll take every suitable fence in the field. If your sister agrees, of course." He straightened, turning his gaze again on Harriet with a conspiratorial smile. "What d'you think, Lady Harriet? Shall we try the fences as a family? Your brother told me of your fondness for the hunt."

Harriet had decided to preserve her own cover by appearing to know nothing at all about the Earl. She said with credible surprise, "You were acquainted with Nicholas, sir?"

"Yes, indeed. Did you not know?" He sounded surprised, shooting a questioning glance at the Duke.

"Oh, surely I told you, Harriet," Lionel said. "Nick brought Lord Marbury to Charlbury several years ago, and they were frequent visitors until the damned war took Nicholas away. The Earl has a standing invitation to visit whenever he wishes, and I issued a most pressing invitation that he join us for Christmas."

"You didn't tell me, sir," she responded, even as she thought, *Two years. Nick had been bringing Marbury to Charlbury for two years and never said a word about him.* She thought she had known most of her brother's close friends.

She smiled easily. "I daresay it was never relevant when I was visiting." She continued swiftly, "But of course, I'm delighted that we shall have a good friend of Nick's with us. It's the first Christmas without him, you understand, my lord." She managed a wan smile.

"I can be no substitute, ma'am," he said quietly. "But we *were* very great friends, and I have many treasured memories, as I'm sure you do."

He sounded so sincere, his gaze was so warm, so private, that for a moment she felt as if he were drawing her into a very particular world that only they could share. Fortunately, the children's clamor of excitement at the Earl's offer gave her a breathing space. He turned to them, solemnly answering the flood of questions about his own hunting experiences, exhibiting all of the patience Nick would have shown, and it increased the strange, disoriented feeling. If she hadn't known what she knew about the man, she would have found him almost irresistibly appealing.

She said abruptly, "I forgot to ask if you have sufficient ink and quills for your correspondence, sir?"

He looked a little startled at this sudden non sequitur but answered calmly enough. "I believe so, ma'am. I must admit I haven't had need of them thus far, so I have not really noticed."

And that was an out-and-out lie, she thought with a little prickle of satisfaction that restored her equanimity somewhat. It was a pointless lie, too, unless he had something to hide. "Well, should that change, Mallow will take your letters to the post every afternoon, if you care to leave them on the pier table by the front door."

"I will remember that, but I doubt very much I will have such a need, Lady Harriet. A man would have to be a churl to prefer writing inanities to distant acquaintances to spending time in such charming company." The black eyes had an almost velvety lustre, and she was aware of a little frisson of something like anticipation.

He was far too attractive for anyone's good, she decided. Had he worked this magic on Nicholas? It seemed out of character to think of Nick telling this man intimate facts about his brother and sisters and yet never mentioning the Earl to herself. He must have trusted him, and she had always considered her brother to be a good judge of character. But, of course, developing trust in one's quarry was how the men in that business operated. Nicholas had probably done the same on occasion, led some trusting soul up a weedy garden path.

She felt the familiar burn of futile anger in the pit of her stomach. Such a waste. First their father and then Nicholas, sacrificed on the altar of patriotism.

And here she was doing much the same. *Set a thief to catch a thief,* she thought with a grim inner smile.

The library doors opened, and Mallow announced, "Dinner is served, your grace."

The twins leaped to their feet. "I'm ravenous," Tom declared. "I could eat a whole sheep and six chickens."

"So could I," Grace added, making for the door.

"Just a minute." Harriet grabbed them both by the arm as they raced past her. "Where are your manners? You don't go in front of the Duke, you know that."

They fell back, looking rather crestfallen, as their grandfather heaved himself from his chair. "It's time Tom was sent to school," he stated. "They'll soon beat some manners into him at Westminster."

Harriet shot him a look half protest, half plea. She had begged for time for Tom to get over losing his father and his beloved brother in the space of two years before he was packed off into the brutal world of Westminster School, and the Duke had reluctantly agreed, but she had no idea how much longer she could hold her ground, and the more unruly Tom was, the more likely his grandfather would insist on his going sooner rather than later.

"An empty belly can cause forgetfulness, sir," the Earl said lightly. "May I offer you my arm?"

"No . . . no, give it to Harriet." The Duke waved a hand in an irritable gesture of dismissal. "We're dining in the yellow salon. I don't want those brats creating havoc in the dining room."

"Oh, dear," Harriet murmured as her grandfather stalked from the library. "Tom . . . Grace, just try not to say anything for a while. Sit still, keep your hands in your laps unless you're eating, and eat slowly. Don't gobble, and don't grab." She pushed them in front of her.

"Turkeys gobble," Grace said, seizing her brother's hand. "Children don't." She tugged Tom to the door.

"For some reason, she always has to have the last word." Harriet shook her head in resignation. "I'm surprised the Duke invited them downstairs tonight. Normally, he wouldn't think of it when we have guests."

"Perhaps he doesn't think of me as a guest," Julius suggested, offering his arm. "And perhaps soon you will not, either. Shall we, ma'am?"

Harriet laid her hand on his arm, annoyed that she could come up with no suitably repressive response. To her relief, the Duke seemed to have recovered his good humor as they took their places around the table in the yellow salon. It was a more intimate setting than the dining hall, where forty covers could be laid comfortably under the brilliant light from the succession of chandeliers. The Duke sat at the head of the oval table, Harriet on his right, Grace next to her. The Earl took his place on the Duke's left, with Tom beside him. The twins hated to be separated, but they were sufficiently subdued to accept their places without protest.

"So you've been at Charlbury for a week, my lord?" Harriet observed, taking up her soupspoon.

"His grace was kind enough to invite me for an extended stay," he replied, deftly sliding Tom's neglected napkin onto the boy's lap just as Harriet was about to remind the child.

"And very good company you are," Lionel declared, taking a sip of his wine with a considering frown. "This is the '67, Mallow?"

"Indeed, sir. As you ordered." The butler lifted the decanter. "I thought it robust enough for the shoulder of mutton . . ." A question mark lingered.

The Duke inhaled the bouquet, took another sip, then nodded. "Yes, definitely. How many bottles do we have?"

"Six cases, sir. If your grace recalls, your grace laid it down just after Lord Edward went away to school."

A spasm crossed the Duke's face at this mention of his dead son. "I recall," he said shortly. "How many guests are you expecting tomorrow, Harriet?"

"I followed your list to the letter, sir." She buttered a roll. "We will be forty in all. Great-aunt Augusta is expected before noon tomorrow. I understand she's staying overnight with her friends in Witney. She prefers to do the journey in easy stages."

"Milksop," Lady Augusta's brother muttered with a derisive sniff. "The woman's ten years younger than I am. Can't think why we had to invite her, anyway."

"We do have to have a nominal hostess, sir," Harriet reminded him.

"Can't think why. You're perfectly capable . . . do all the work as it is."

"Yes, sir, but I am neither married nor a widow. People would talk." He knew this perfectly well and, she suspected, would have been horrified if she had suggested such a breach of convention herself, but the Duke found his sister a serious irritant. She made much of what she insisted on calling her frail constitution, even while consuming large quantities of sweetmeats and glasses of ratafia while languishing upon a daybed among paisley shawls and bottles of sal volatile.

Julius stepped smoothly into the momentary tense silence with a question to the Duke about the coverts, and Harriet gratefully continued with her dinner, monitoring the twins as she did so. They were hungry enough to concentrate mostly on their plates, and the meal passed without further incident. The first cover was replaced with a Rhenish cream and a basket of macaroons, and harmony continued to reign.

When they had finished, she put aside her napkin. "If you'll excuse us, gentlemen, we'll leave you to your port. It's time the children were in bed."

"We're not tired," Tom protested.

"No, not in the least," Grace stated. "I haven't yawned once."

"Nevertheless, Nurse Maddox will be waiting for you. Say good night." Harriet rose from the table, and reluctantly the twins followed suit. They dutifully bade their grandfather and his guest good night, and their sister hustled them out of the salon.

"We'll repair to the library soon, my dear," Lionel said. "We'll take tea there."

"I'll be down shortly." She propelled the children past the footman holding the door and hurried them up to the nursery floor, where she left them in the charge of their nurse and her underlings.

"We're going to ride our ponies tomorrow, Harry," Tom informed her as she kissed him good night.

"Yes, we have to practice before the hunt," Grace said. "Just riding in the park in town isn't as exciting as riding across the fields and jumping the hedges, is it?" Her voice was muffled as one of the nursemaids lifted her muslin dress over her head.

"No, probably not," Harriet agreed. "We must hope it's a fine day tomorrow." She blew them a final kiss and left the nursery with a sense of liberation. An entire day in the twins' close company was quite exhausting. She went to her own chamber before continuing downstairs. Agnes was passing a copper warming pan between the sheets as Harriet came in.

"Oh, m'lady, are you coming to bed now?"

"No, no, not yet, Agnes. In an hour, perhaps." She sat at the dresser and adjusted her hair, repositioning a couple of pins that had worked loose, before going down to the library. It was empty, the men were still sitting over their port, but Mallow had brought in the tea tray, and she sat by the fire, poured herself a cup, and took up a copy of the *Morning Gazette*. She had read only a few lines when the door opened.

"Ah, Lady Harriet . . . did the children go to bed

without complaint?" The Earl smiled as he came over to the fire.

"I left before they could start complaining," she said, pouring tea and handing him the cup. "Did you leave the Duke at the table?"

"No, he said he was fatigued and was going straight upstairs. I was to wish you a good night. He will see you at breakfast, 'without the brats,' and I quote." He sat opposite her and took a sip of tea, still smiling at her over the lip.

"He puts on a pretense of finding them annoying, but generally, they amuse him as long as they don't get under his feet," she said, wondering why she felt a little quavery, as if she were nervous about something. It couldn't be because she was alone with the man, surely?

"I rather thought so. But what of you, Lady Harriet? It must be quite a burden to assume the day-to-day responsibility for such a lively pair?" He sounded genuinely concerned, genuinely interested, and his eyes were on her again with that warm glow that made her feel oddly special.

"It was certainly easier when Nick was around," she replied, carefully folding the *Gazette,* using the task to conceal her strange agitation. "We had responsibility for them, really, since they were born. Our mother died in childbirth, and our father was not around very often. He seemed content to leave them in the nursery and let them grow as they would." She shrugged a little, laying the newspaper on the table beside the tea tray. "It's not an unusual way of parenting, but Nick and I were more interested in them, we felt an obligation, and it grew from that."

"It must be doubly hard for you now, then?"

"Yes," she said bluntly. "You say you knew Nick well?"

"As well as I've ever known anyone," he responded.

"How did you meet?" she asked casually, pouring herself more tea. How would he answer? Not with the truth, she was sure.

"In Paris," he answered. "At a soiree given by the Countess de Fauviere. We discovered we had some interests in common and grew to enjoy each other's company."

"How long ago was that?" She leaned back in her chair, her senses alert even as her voice remained casual, as if the conversation were only mildly interesting.

He frowned, stretching his long legs to the fire. "About two years ago, I think."

"Strange he never mentioned your name," she mused. "If you were that close. We never had secrets from each other." *Except, of course, that he never mentioned his clandestine work until he'd taken that last mission . . . the mission that had ended with his death.*

A slight, chilly smile touched his mouth. "Perhaps I thought the relationship more important than he did."

"Or perhaps Nick considered it too important to share, even with me." She couldn't help the retort, although she instantly wished it unsaid.

"Well, we'll never know," Julius said, his tone once again light and easy. "Even those we know well can behave in mysterious ways."

"I'm sure you're right." She set her cup down, preparing to get up.

"The family resemblance is quite remarkable, you know."

The comment kept her in her seat. "In what way?"

He laughed. "My dear, the hair color, the green eyes, the shape of the nose . . . all four of you. A man would have to be blind not to know you as siblings. You all take after your grandfather."

"Maybe so. The portraits in the Long Gallery might prove your point." She rose from her seat. "If you'll excuse me, sir, it's been a long and tiring day."

"Of course." He rose with alacrity. "If you have time in the morning, perhaps we could take a stroll in the Long Gallery and look at some of the family portraits. I own I would be very interested to trace the resemblance."

"If I have time, of course," she responded. "But the guests arrive tomorrow, and I daresay I shall be very busy. However, please feel free to take a look yourself."

"But I would not enjoy it nearly so much without your company." He accompanied her into the hall and to the foot of the stairs. He lit a carrying candle from the thick wax taper beside the night-lights and gave it to her, his fingers brushing lightly against hers. His eyes seemed to see right into her, and again she felt that sense of being caught in their own universe.

"Good night, Lady Harriet." His hand fell from hers, but his eyes remained upon hers as he made a slight bow.

"Good night, Lord Marbury." She sketched a curtsy and swept away up the stairs, her free hand resting on the banister.

Julius watched her go, a little smile playing over his mouth. She was all and more than he had expected from Nick's glowing descriptions. But something was not quite right. Unless he was much mistaken, she seemed suspicious of him for some reason. But why? He was simply a Christmas guest, a friend of her brother's, invited by her grandfather. It felt as if she had taken an instant dislike to him, but as far as he knew, he had done nothing to warrant it.

And just why had she been hovering outside his bedchamber door? For a moment, she had looked as guilty as sin when he'd accosted her, but why? Maybe he *had* been a little sarcastic, but then, he didn't like being surprised.

He shrugged and returned to the library. If his manner had caused her to take offense, he would do what he could on the morrow to remedy it. He would go about his own business in the afternoon, when his absence would not be remarked amidst the flurry of arrivals.

Chapter Three

Harriet entered her bedchamber with the sense of achieving sanctuary. Every minute in the Earl's company that evening had put her on edge. She had to be on her guard. He mustn't suspect her of taking any unusual interest in him, but foolishly, she hadn't expected to find such constant vigilance so exhausting. However, she didn't think she'd slipped up so far.

"Shall I help you to bed, m'lady?" Agnes jumped up from an ottoman in front of the fire, where she'd been waiting for her ladyship.

"Just help me into my night robe and brush my hair, and then you may fetch me up a glass of warm milk with a little brandy and go to your own bed,

Agnes." She began to unpin her hair, running her fingers through it to loosen the tight knots.

Agnes unbuttoned and unlaced her gown and helped her into the muslin nightgown and warm velvet robe before taking up the ivory-backed brush and beginning to draw it through Harriet's wheat-colored hair, which now hung in a shining curtain to below her shoulders. It was a little darker than the twins', Harriet thought, watching the candlelight catch the reddish tint amidst the fair strands. But their heads would darken as they grew older, just as hers and Nick's had.

A sense of loss washed through her as she thought of her brother, saw in her mind's eye the lively sparkle in his green eyes, the little hazel glints in the background. She heard his voice as clearly as if he were in the room with her, sitting as he so often did astride a chair, his arms resting along its back, chatting with her as she got ready for the evening.

Had Julius Forsythe been instrumental in Nick's murder? If Harriet could find one piece of incontrovertible evidence during these twelve days when she and the Earl were under the same roof, it would be over. The whole wretched mystery, the twists and turns . . . over. And she could grieve for her brother's death without any of the questions and ambiguities that made simple grief so difficult to embrace.

"Is everything all right, ma'am? Do you feel quite well?" Agnes's concerned voice interrupted her reverie.

She managed a smile. "Yes . . . yes, of course. I am quite well. I was just thinking about something." She must learn to school her countenance, she thought guiltily. How could she expect to fool as skillful and experienced a spy as Julius Forsythe if her expression revealed her thoughts to an innocent child like Agnes?

"You seemed sad, ma'am."

"A little, perhaps. That will be all for now. You should seek your bed."

"I'll fetch up your milk, then, my lady." Agnes set down the brush on the dresser and hurried to the door.

Harriet remained at the dresser, examining her reflection critically. Her green eyes, flecked like Nick's with hazel, were large and luminous, something she had always valued, but now she thought it a grave disadvantage. They were far too expressive for a spy. And her creamy pallor was far too quick to flush up with anger or embarrassment. A positive curse in the present business. How did one control these natural responses?

She got up restlessly and walked to the window, moving the heavy velvet curtain aside. The glass panes were freezing, needles of cold air creeping around the window frame. Shielding her eyes, she pressed her forehead against the glass. A few faint specks of white were drifting against the darkness. The twins would be ecstatic if it really snowed, but it would play havoc for their guests in the morning, making already tedious journeys utterly miserable.

"'Tis snowing, m'lady." Agnes's voice, sounding almost jubilant, came from the room behind her, and Harriet backed out, letting the curtain fall again.

"Yes, so I see."

"Oh, I do 'ope we 'as a white Christmas, my lady. My brothers and me, we love to 'ave snowball fights."

Harriet laughed. "Yes, we used to as well. And the twins will be over the moon if it settles." *But maybe it won't,* she thought to herself. It was a shame to be so grown up that one wished away snow over Christmas, but that was the reality. And the Duke would be mad as fire if snow prevented the Boxing Day hunt.

Agnes set down the silver tray with a glass of hot

milk and a plate of mince pies on a low table by the fireside chair. "Will that be all, then, ma'am?"

"Yes, thank you. Go to your bed now, and wake me at eight in the morning, if you please."

Agnes bobbed a curtsy and disappeared with a murmured good night. Harriet sat down by the fire, taking up her drink with a smile of pleasure. These quiet moments before bed were her favorite time of the day, when she could reflect on the day's happenings and contemplate the morrow. It would be a busy day, and somehow, in all the bustle, she must manage to field the twins while keeping a close but covert eye on the Earl of Marbury.

For some reason, she found the prospect of the latter task rather appealing, for all the anxiety it caused her. She seemed to take a perverse pleasure in his company, even as the strain of watching her every move and expression grew stronger. It was most inconvenient—so much simpler to find him distasteful, unpleasantly arrogant or secretive, or just plain unattractive. And yet he was none of those things, at least not on the surface. He actually seemed to enjoy the children's company, which in itself was sufficiently unusual to be interesting. In Harriet's experience, bachelors of the Earl's means and stature barely noticed children, let alone bothered to gain their confidence.

Had Nick really liked him? Had he trusted him? She sipped her milk and frowned into the fire. She no longer found it surprising that Nick had never mentioned Julius to her. They were engaged together in the same clandestine work, and Nick had been involved in the covert world for at least a year before he had told Harriet about it.

Just before he had gone on his last mission, just after Spain had declared war on England . . . she remembered she had been picking grapes in the hot house at Charlbury to send to London as a present for her old governess, when Nick had come into the damp, overheated conservatory. He was on leave before shipping out, and she was already steeling herself for the moment of good-bye. She had looked up at him, brushing a damp tendril of hair from her eyes, smiling at him through the misty atmosphere. But his expression had been oddly somber, she remembered, and when he had spoken, his voice had been barely above a whisper.

He had told her he was leaving Charlbury that night, heading for Dover, where he would take a fishing boat to France. Apart from his masters, only she was to know that he was not leaving with his regiment.

Harriet had listened at first in disbelief, thinking he was playing some strange joke upon her, but Nick was not one for practical jokes. Slowly, she understood exactly what he was telling her. Her brother was a spy. It was expected that France, under the military leadership of Bonaparte, would soon begin planning an invasion of Britain, and Nick was to go to France to join up with an intelligence network along the Brittany coast, from where they would pass information back to their country. He needed a safe address outside the usual intelligence channels to send his coded information, and he wanted his sister to act as his poste restante. She would not be involved in any danger; the coded information would be included within the ordinary letters he sent her as a matter of course. The letters would travel on the packet boats with the routine mail just as always, and they should attract no particular attention from anyone watching the mails for suspicious activity. She would be contacted in the London house in order to pass on the correspondence.

Harriet would never refuse her brother anything, and it hadn't occurred to her to refuse him then, however astonishing the request and what it revealed about her best friend. It was a simple enough part to play, after all.

It seemed oddly naïve now, how easily she had agreed, Harriet thought. But then, she had been infected by Nick's enthusiasm for his role, by the power of a patriotism that could actually manifest itself in some concrete fashion. They had been full of excitement, thrilled at the prospect of working together for their country.

She had seen her brother ride off in the dark hour before dawn . . . and she had never seen him again.

Oh, the letters had come as he had said they would, and George Howard, an unremarkable dapper gentleman looking like a man of business, had paid regular visits to Devere House in London to receive them.

Then the letters had ceased.

She had waited in an agony of anxiety until Howard had come to tell her that Nicholas had been killed in the siege of Elba, and the next morning, his name had appeared among the war dead in the *London Gazette*. And until that morning in November when Howard and Bedford had visited her in London and told her the truth, she had been left alone with her grief, concentrating on the children, who needed every moment of her time. They had adored Nick, and their own uncomprehending grief had expressed itself in alternating outbursts of rage and long periods of sullen and uncooperative silence. The war in Europe had continued, with shifting alliances, treaties made and broken, and all the while, the threat of the French invasion grew more powerful.

But things had changed that November morning. If what the men from the Ministry suspected was true, then Julius Forsythe had been using his friendship with Nicholas Devere to betray his own country. And eventually, he had betrayed Nicholas. As Harriet had absorbed this implication, a deep, cold rage had entered her soul, almost superseding her grief. She would be avenged. If this man had been responsible for Nick's murder in a back alley, he would pay, and she would ensure that he did.

The twins no longer needed her single-minded attention; they missed their brother, but they were coming out of the worst of their grief. In essence, it was not a difficult task the men were asking of her, just simple observation.

But now Harriet felt the need to take things further, to dig deeper. She had been intrigued by the indentations on the vellum at the Earl's secretaire, by the way he had burned the paper, and particularly by the lie he had told about having no need to do correspondence on this holiday visit. She could simply report that to her contacts and leave the rest to them, but her need for vengeance would not be satisfied by such a passive role. The man who had been responsible for Nick's death had wormed his way into the affections of her grandfather and had gained the confidence of the children. It was up to her now to expose him for what he was—and as soon as possible. Neither the Duke nor the children should have to bear another loss.

He would be joining the gentlemen in their various sporting pursuits during the following days, and there would be opportunity aplenty for a thorough investigation of his chamber and possessions.

Harriet yawned and drained her glass. She snuffed the candles on the mantel and took herself to bed, leaning out to blow the bedside taper before burrowing down into the deep feather mattress behind the thick, sheltering bedcurtains.

Julius Forsythe was sitting at the desk in his bedchamber as the house slept around him. Thomas had long since helped him into his night robe, poured him a generous measure of cognac, and left him to go to his own bed, but Julius preferred the night hours for some of the more intellectually demanding aspects of his work. The crackle of the log in the hearth, the occasional creak of a floorboard, and the scuttle of a mouse were the only sounds apart from the scratch of his pen on the vellum.

Lines of letters and numbers appeared beneath his quill, he made swift notations in the margins, and he occasionally consulted a volume of Chaucer's *Canterbury Tales* in the original Middle English as he decoded the hieroglyphics on the small scrap of paper that had reached him via a carrier pigeon the day before. His response would go on its way by the same method from a pigeon loft in Turl Street in Oxford the following afternoon.

A slight smile touched his lips as he thought of Harriet and her solicitous information about leaving his mail on the pier table in the hall for the butler. He hadn't lied when he said he had no need of such a conventional means of transmitting correspondence.

His pen paused as he looked up from his work, momentarily distracted by the mental image of Lady Harriet Devere. She was certainly very like Nicholas and yet also in very important ways most unlike him. Her eyes were larger, he thought, maybe a deeper shade of green, and the reddish glints in her wheat-colored hair were almost an indefinable color, sometimes pink, sometimes almost copper when the light fell upon her head in a certain fashion.

She had a much fuller mouth than her brother, he remembered, but the straight nose and high cheek-bones were the same, definitely a family trait, particularly pronounced in the old Duke. He liked the way she carried herself, with the cool assurance of one confident of who she was and where she fitted in her world. And in that, she most resembled Lord Hesketh.

Nicholas had borne himself with supreme confidence but never without thought. It was what had made him so valuable at his work. He examined every aspect of a situation, every angle of a plan, an ability that Julius admired and had himself in abundance. It was what made them such a superb partnership, until it had to end in that wretched way. A knife to the throat in a back alley was no way for a man like Nicholas to die. And yet sometimes it was inevitable. It had been inevitable that Nicholas Devere should die like that.

Julius shook his head briskly, as if to dispel cob-webs, dipped his quill into the ink, and continued with his work.

Chapter Four

Harriet woke just before Agnes came in with her morning chocolate. She hitched herself up against the pillows as her maid drew back the bedcurtains.

"It's stopped snowing, m'lady, just a dusting on the ground," Agnes informed her, setting the tray on the coverlet before going to draw back the curtains to let in the daylight. Crisp sunlight shone through the frosted windowpanes.

"It looks like a good day for traveling," Harriet observed with a degree of relief, drawing a cashmere shawl around her shoulders against the chill air.

"I'll have the fire blazin' quick as a flash, ma'am." Agnes bent to poke the dying embers before adding fresh kindling and new logs. "Will you be goin' down for breakfast, m'lady, or should I bring up a tray?"

"No, I'll breakfast with the Duke in the breakfast parlor." Harriet poured a fragrant stream of chocolate into her cup from the silver pot. Presumably, the Earl would also be joining them. "I'll wear the green muslin morning gown, Agnes." The decision followed her previous thought. People told her she looked particularly fetching in green, and her mission was to charm the Earl, after all, to slip beneath his guard if she could. If it meant she should look her best at all times in his company, and looking her best always made her sparkle, so be it. She sipped her chocolate, the crackle of the logs as they caught in the hearth making the room feel warm and welcoming again.

Half an hour later, she descended to the breakfast parlor and was surprised and, she had to admit, a little disappointed to find only her grandfather at the table. He looked up from the journal he was reading and nodded at her. "Good morning, Harriet. You slept well, I trust."

"As always, sir. I find Charlbury very conducive to a peaceful night." She glanced at his tankard and without comment refilled it from the jug on the table. "Can I fetch you something from the sideboard?"

He examined his plate with an air of mild curiosity. "To tell you the truth, I can't even remember what I was eating. There's a most interesting article in the journal about this man Jenner. He calls this treatment for smallpox *vaccination,* apparently deriving from the Latin *vacca,* for a cow. He injects patients with cowpox, and somehow it inoculates them against the disease." He peered at his granddaughter. "I shall look into it further. If it works, then everyone on the estate must receive this protection, and you and the children most particularly."

Harriet smiled a vague acknowledgment, not at all sure quite how to respond. It was never wise to disagree with the Duke when he had taken to an idea, but she had her doubts about sticking needles into the twins, let alone the superstitious folks on the estate. It would come under the heading of witchcraft, she rather suspected. Tom and Grace would object at the top of their lungs.

She helped herself to eggs. "His lordship is not joining us?"

"He's probably out around the estate. He's a keen sportsman . . . just like Nicholas." The Duke cleared his throat, then returned to his journal.

Harriet took a chair at the table and buttered a

piece of toast. She knew better than to interrupt her grandfather when he was reading and instead turned her thoughts to the day ahead. After breakfast, she must look over the menus with Cook and Mrs. Sutcliff . . . A gleeful shout from beyond the French windows brought her head up swiftly. She looked over at the windows, which opened onto the frost-sparkling lawns at the rear of the house. The twins were prancing outside, waving and shrieking with laughter, while Tess, the retriever, jumped up at them, barking and wagging her tail, obviously enjoying the game. Behind them came the tall figure of Julius Forsythe, tossing a ball between his gloved hands.

"What on earth is going on?" Lionel demanded, staring over the top of his paper.

"I'm not sure." Harriet went to open the French windows. "Come in quickly, before you let all the cold air in."

"We were playing football, Harry!" Tom shouted as he catapulted through the door.

"Yes, and I scored a goal, didn't I, sir?" Grace cried, at a pitch rivaling her brother's. "And then we found enough snow for a snowball fight."

"Yes, and we fought against Lord Marbury, and—"

"Pipe down, the pair of you." Their grandfather's bellow cut Tom off in midspeech, and they both fell into openmouthed silence.

"You may blame me, sir, for the excitement." The Earl stepped into the room and closed the doors behind him. "Sit, Tess. Heel." He gestured sharply to the retriever, who was still bouncing around the children. The dog sat obediently at his feet.

"I fail to see why you should be held responsible for this unruly pair's ill manners," the Duke said testily.

"Nevertheless, Duke, I am responsible for encouraging a rather lively game." Julius's smile was a little rueful as he bowed to Harriet. "Lady Harriet, I hope I may be forgiven."

"I know my brother and sister far too well to hold you to blame, sir," Harriet returned with an answering smile that came all too easily. "It takes nothing to get them excited—a dog, a ball, and an element of competition will do it anytime." She turned to the twins. "You had best go up and find Nurse Maddox. I'm sure she'll be looking for you."

"Off you go," the Earl said quietly, turning them to the door when they hesitated. "Let your grandfather continue with his breakfast in peace." He shooed them from the room, closing the door behind them, then stood with that same rueful smile, tossing the ball from one hand to the other.

"Have you breakfasted, sir?"

"Not as yet. I saw the children from my bedchamber window and was struck with the urge to kick a ball around." He gave a self-deprecating laugh. "I can't think what came over me."

"Neither can I," muttered the Duke. "Sit down, man. Take a tankard of ale, and Harriet will fetch you a plate of kidneys . . . or kippers, if you prefer."

"Or both," Harriet said, regarding him with a raised eyebrow as she stood at the chafing dishes on the sideboard.

"Kippers first, then, thank you." He sat down at the table. "It's a lovely morning, but the ground's like iron. It was quite a frost last night."

The Duke looked concerned. "Not too hard for the horses, I trust. I'd best talk to Jackson about the hunt." He set his paper aside and stood. "If you'll both excuse me. I'll see you later, Marbury. Harriet, send for me as soon as Augusta arrives, will you? She'll sulk for hours if I'm not there to bid her welcome."

"Of course." Harriet hid a smile as her grandfather strode from the breakfast parlor. She set a plate of kippers in front of the Earl and took her own seat, buttering a piece of toast. "He'll be badgering poor Jackson morning, noon, and night now until the hunt."

"Jackson?"

"The Huntsman. It'll be up to him to make the decision about going out on Boxing Day." Harriet sipped coffee. "It was kind of you to give the children your time this morning."

"*Kind.* Good God, I wasn't kicking a ball with them out of kindness, I assure you." He sounded genuinely offended. "It reminded me of impromptu games in my childhood. My brother and I used to play with the village lads when we could escape surveillance." He dissected his kipper with meticulous delicacy.

"Well, I am grateful, anyway. They need some attention from someone other than myself. Tom, in particular, needs some . . ." Her voice faded. How to say that Tom needed a man's influence, a man's attention, now that his own brother and father were no longer there to provide it?

"Yes, I understand," the Earl said swiftly. "It's hard for a lad to grow up under a petticoat regime, however sporting and indulgent it may be." He gave her a swift smile. "You can't expect to replace Nicholas, my dear girl."

She felt her cheeks warm. "I don't." And now all

she could think was that this man, offering these comforting nuggets of understanding, was suspected of being responsible for Nick's death, even if he had not actually wielded the knife himself. And maybe he had. No one had seen the killing. She dropped her eyes, knowing they would reveal too much, and pushed back her chair, abandoning her toast. "If you'll excuse me, my lord, I have much to do this morning before the guests arrive. I'm sure you are sufficiently at home here to entertain yourself."

He rose with her, bowing, his face expressionless, his dark eyes unreadable. "As you say." As she reached the door, he said, "I am still hoping for a tour of the picture gallery at some point, if you should manage to find the time."

Harriet reminded herself that she would get nowhere by holding him at arm's length. She raised her eyes to meet his steady gaze. "In an hour, perhaps. I will meet you in the Long Gallery, sir."

"I look forward to it." He bowed again as she whisked herself from the room.

Thoughtfully, Julius returned to his neglected kipper. What had been behind that sudden withdrawal? One minute she had been all conspiratorial smiles, and the next cold and distant. The instant before she had lowered her eyes, he had caught a sudden burn of anger, but he couldn't imagine what he might have done or said to cause it. Nicholas had not had a mercurial temperament, he reflected. And as far as he could remember, in his many descriptions of his beloved sister, Nick had never so much as hinted at anything but an intelligent, humorous equanimity.

He shook his head and drank his ale. He had little time for the fair sex in his life, and while he'd had his liaisons, brief encounters over the years, he had never really spent concerted time with any one woman. He was never in one place long enough . . . or so he had always thought. The novel thought occurred now that perhaps he simply hadn't met a woman who would make staying around worthwhile. He frowned at the pile of fish bones on his plate. How would he know when, or rather if, he did meet such a woman? His eyes drifted towards the closed door. Then he shook his head again in a gesture of mild exasperation and reached for the ale jug to refill his tankard.

Harriet fought to concentrate on the business in hand as she met with Cook and the housekeeper, discussing the various merits of a baron of beef versus a boar's head for the Christmas table and the need for calves'-foot jelly for Great-aunt Augusta, who would insist upon it even though she barely touched it. "Oh, and we must make sure to have plenty of your cheese tartlets for Lord Howarth, Cook. You know how much he likes them."

"Oh, aye, right partial to 'em, he is," Cook said with a complacent smile. "And there'll be partridge pies an' veal and ham for the shooting-party lunch."

"Have the children been down yet to stir the puddings?" Stirring the Christmas puddings was a childhood ritual, and Harriet remembered how it had felt to stand up on a high stool at the massive kitchen table, struggling with the great wooden ladle to mix the bowl of candied fruits, nuts, eggs, suet, flour, and whatever else Cook had decided to add, her nose tickling with the powerful fumes of the brandy that was slurped in at every turn. Nick had always sneaked a finger around the edge of the bowl to taste the mixture when no one was looking. The brandy had always made him choke. She gave herself a mental shake.

"They'll be down this afternoon to do that, an'

tomorrow afternoon when the cake and that fancy *bouchedenoel,* or however them Frenchies call it . . . can't think what's wrong with a good old-fashioned Christmas cake." She sniffed. "When they've been iced, the children can come and decorate them. I'll be making the marzipan today."

"I know you will achieve your usual magic, Cook." Harriet checked the last item on her list. "I think that's all, unless you have any questions."

"No, that'll do for me, my lady." Cook brushed off her immaculate starched white apron. "I'll be back to me kitchen now." She bobbed a curtsy and rustled out.

"Will you be able to manage without Doris, Mrs. Sutcliff?"

"It's to be hoped we won't have too many young ladies without their own maids," the housekeeper replied.

"Well, I'm sure I can manage without Agnes waiting upon me all the time, so if there are any, you may send Agnes to them." Harriet nodded a pleasant dismissal, hoping to cut off any objections from the housekeeper, who looked as if she were ready to launch into a catalogue of complaints.

"Well, if you say so, m'lady." Mrs. Sutcliff inclined her head in a stiff curtsy and sailed from Harriet's parlor.

Harriet leaned back in her chair and exhaled with relief. That was the worst of the morning's tasks taken care of. She could safely leave the management of the household to those who understood it best. It was purely for form's sake that she involved herself at all. She glanced at the clock. It was almost ten, nearly an hour since she'd left the Earl in the breakfast parlor. He would be expecting her in the Long Gallery. Great-aunt Augusta would not arrive much before noon. So what was she waiting for? She rose and headed for the door.

The Earl was ahead of her in the Long Gallery, standing with his hands clasped behind him, examining a portrait of a gentleman in a cartwheel ruff, a gold slashed doublet, and skintight hose that left very little of his masculinity to the imagination.

"The first Earl Devere," Harriet said, coming to stand beside him.

"A remarkably well-endowed gentleman," Julius observed.

Harriet gave an involuntary chuckle. "He definitely has something of a peacock's strut about him. I'm sure he thought himself God's gift to the female sex."

She ought to have ignored the inappropriate comment, but she'd had the same thought many times. "Family history has it that he was a pirate, a bandit, an all-round scoundrel, who did Elizabeth some sterling service, presumably enriching her treasury with his thieving, and she gave him an earldom in return. Charles I conferred the ducal coronet on the fourth Earl."

She moved along the wall, stopping in front of a gentleman in full Cavalier regalia. "He went into exile with Charles II and became known as something of a hell-raiser after the Restoration. Nick and I used to speculate on how many illegitimate children he had and whether there's an entire branch of Fitz Deveres somewhere in the country."

"And is there a portrait of your own father?"

"Yes, over here." She turned and crossed to the opposite side of the gallery. "Our father, Lord Edward, and our mother, Lady Charlotte." She gestured to the two portraits side-by-side.

Julius examined them with his head slightly tilted. "Mmm. As I said before, the Devere family resemblance is very pronounced, but you have your mother's forehead and chin, I believe." He put his hand on her chin and turned her face slightly towards him, regarding her with a quizzical smile. "Yes, most definitely. The widow's peak is exactly your mother's, and this rather stubborn chin." A finger traced the curve of her chin, and then his hand dropped to her shoulder, resting lightly as he continued to scrutinize the portraits, as casually as if he were unaware of it.

Harriet froze beneath the touch. It was warm and light, and one finger moved almost absently up the column of her neck. She wanted to move away, to say something, anything to break this moment of physical contact. But something kept her right where she was, unmoving, feeling the warmth of his hand, the light stroke of his finger along her neck. He said nothing, seemed not to consider his position in the least out of place.

Did he know what he was doing?

"It's strange how I feel I know you, Harriet," he said in the sudden tense silence. "It must be because I knew Nick so well, and you are so very alike." His tone was as light as the caressing finger. "Nick always called you Harry, but perhaps I may not presume that far." He moved his finger to her chin again, turning her face to his. "May I?"

Harriet swallowed, fighting myriad sensations, some

unwelcome, some oddly pleasing, all of them unfamiliar. "No," she said abruptly. "That is a family name, Lord Marbury."

He inclined his head in calm acknowledgment. "I understand. But you will not object to *Harriet*?"

Did she? She shook her head. "Not really. It is my name, after all."

He gave a slightly twisted smile. "Not the wholehearted endorsement I might have wished for. But I'll take what I'm given. You will call me Julius."

It seemed like a command, she thought. "I'll have to see about that, sir. Shall we continue with the tour?" She moved away from him at last, and his hand fell from her shoulder, leaving an oddly cold patch on her skin. "This particular ancestor went to the wars with the Duke of Marlborough."

Julius followed her, wondering a little what he thought he was doing. He hadn't intended to touch her, or even to invite this first-name play, but somehow it had just happened. He was not accustomed to acting on impulse, but he found Harriet Devere a challenge, and he was not in the habit of ignoring challenges. He didn't know why some of the time she seemed to have taken a dislike to him, and at other times her smile, her ready chuckle, the sparkle in the green eyes seemed almost like an invitation.

Oh, yes, she was certainly a challenge, but a most attractive and appealing challenge into the bargain. No wonder he was more than ready to rise to it.

"Where did you say you met Nick?" she asked, coming to a halt in front of the portrait.

"In Paris, two years ago."

"Ah, yes, I remember now." She kept a safe distance between them. "Paris was hardly a comfortable place to visit two years ago."

"No, but the Directory had been appointed, and the Terror was officially over. I was interested in seeing the situation for myself."

"And was that why Nick was there?" She asked the questions casually, trying to conceal her passionate interest in his answers.

"I gather so. He was with a group of curious friends, and we met and took to each other immediately."

"I find it strange that he never mentioned you to me," she observed. "I knew most of his really good friends."

He shrugged, saying with a half laugh, "Well, as I said, perhaps I valued the friendship more than did Nick."

She turned to look at him then, her green gaze

searching. "Nick valued friendships he could trust, sir. He valued openness in his friendships. Perhaps he felt you were withholding something from him?"

His black eyes held hers in a steady gaze for a moment, and then he said, "I have the habit of reticence. Sometimes that impedes as close a friendship as I would like."

It seemed like a confidence, and she was debating how to respond when the sound of carriage wheels on the driveway below broke the instant of silence. "Oh, Lord, that'll be Great-aunt Augusta. I must go down at once."

Julius watched her disappear in a blur of green muslin. He walked to one of the long windows overlooking the drive and stood looking down, stroking his chin thoughtfully. A massive Berlin carriage stood below, six horses in the traces, the roof piled high with luggage. A woman, clearly a lady's maid, judging by her black pelisse and bonnet, was fussing with an armful of shawls at the carriage steps as a lady descended on the arm of a footman, who held a small pug in his other arm. The lady was swathed in furs, batting at the footman with her muff as he tried to take an enormous reticule suspended from her arm. Julius could hear nothing, but he could hazard a guess at the gist

from what he'd heard of Great-aunt Augusta. Harriet
appeared, hurrying down the steps, and surreptitiously
he pushed open the window, leaning close to listen.

"My dear ma'am, you must be frozen," Harriet declared, anticipating the first complaint as she curtsied
to her relative. "There is a good fire going in your
parlor, and hot water for a mustard bath if you feel
you may be catching cold. Dacre, her ladyship's bedchamber is prepared, and if her ladyship should need
a posset, you must send instantly to the kitchen." The
maid disappeared up the stairs in a waft of black taffeta, giving instructions left, right, and center with all
the assurance of one who knows her importance.

"Ah, Harriet . . . there you are at last . . . let go
of my arm, you silly man." Augusta swatted the at-
tendant footman with a degree of vigor. "Take poor
Horace to my chamber, and fetch him some chicken
livers. I am afraid he is catching an ague . . . such a
dreadful, interminable journey. I don't know why we
don't just stay at home, but of course, dear child, I
must do my duty. My dear brother must have a hostess for his endless parties. Now, let me look at you."

A pair of surprisingly sharp green eyes subjected
Harriet to an intent scrutiny. "Well, you don't look
too bad. You've left off mourning, I see."

"It was the Duke's wish, ma'am. Nick has been gone almost a year," Harriet responded. She had been prepared for this, and the sooner it was over and done with, the better. "Will you come inside? The Duke will be waiting to welcome you."

"Well, where is he, then?" The lady raised a lorgnette to her eyes and looked pointedly around. "Can't be troubled to come to the door, I see."

"He was with his estate manager, ma'am. He asked to be informed the moment you arrived," Harriet said soothingly. "Please come inside out of the cold."

Her ladyship allowed herself to be ushered up the steps into the house. As Harriet set foot on the bottom step, something drew her eyes upwards. Julius, standing at an open window of the Long Gallery, touched his forehead in a mock salute of congratulation, and there was something about the accompanying smile that seemed once again to include her in their own private circle.

A little chill ran down her spine. It was how she and Nick had been. Negotiating their way through the family maze, sharing their own private jokes. But she couldn't have that with anyone else. Most particularly not with Julius Forsythe.

Chapter Five

The bustle of arrivals continued for the next several hours. Julius kept to the sidelines, watching with considerable respect the deft way Harriet managed to be everywhere at once, solving problems, smoothing ruffled tempers, instructing servants, even as she deflected the more outrageous demands and complaints of Aunt Augusta and several other imperious dowagers, whose personal maids appeared more demanding even than their mistresses.

"Good God, man, come into the library, it's the only sane place in the entire house," the Duke declared, entering the hall after welcoming a trio of gentlemen guests. "Don't know why we have to do this every year, but Harriet insists upon it . . . says it's our duty to the family." He gave a snort of disapproval. "Come and join me in a glass of port, dear fellow."

He took Julius's arm and ushered him swiftly into the library, closing the door behind them with a sigh of relief. "Oh, good, Harriet's made sure we've some nourishment in here." He gestured to a sideboard where a cold ham, smoked trout, and a loaf of wheat bread reposed beside decanters of port and claret. "The red salon will be full of gannets eating me out of house and home," he announced, filling two glasses with port. "Bad enough to have their incessant chatter over dinner, without having to endure it in the middle of the day."

Julius took the glass with a smile of thanks. "You really dislike Christmas festivities that much, Duke?"

The Duke gave a wry grimace. "I suppose I was overstating the case, somewhat. The first day is always the worst; once everyone settles in, it isn't so bad. Harriet achieves miracles, don't know how she does it, just a slip of a girl." He sipped his port and turned to the sideboard. "Help yourself, dear boy. We won't dine until seven tonight, after the carolers have come up from the village." He piled a plate with the offerings on the sideboard and carried it to a fireside chair.

Julius followed suit. The library was an oasis of peace and quiet amidst the noise and bustle of the house. "Any word on the Boxing Day hunt, sir?"

The Duke looked much more cheerful. "Yes, indeed, we are in luck. Jackson thinks the ground will be fine if we don't get another hard frost." He took a hearty bite of bread and ham.

Julius glanced towards the window, where weak sunlight sparked off the still frosty lawn. The long case clock chimed one o'clock. It would be almost dusk in three hours, and he needed to ride into Oxford and back before full dark. He set down his plate and glass. "If you'll excuse me, sir, I've a mind to ride out for a couple of hours. My horse has been eating his head off in the stables for the last couple of days, and if he's to be fit to hunt, he'll need to work out the fidgets."

"Of course, dear boy. Go with my blessing. I only wish I could accompany you, but Harriet will frown if I leave before the last guest arrives." His grace shook his head with a mock mournful air. "In truth, I owe it to her to stay around at least for today. Augusta will demand my presence soon enough."

Julius laughed sympathetically as he rose to his feet. "I'll bid you good afternoon, then."

"The carolers assemble in the great hall at six," his

host reminded him. "Harriet will not be best pleased if you miss them."

"I will be there, sir. I wouldn't wish to displease Lady Harriet." *Rather the reverse,* he thought with an inner smile. He bowed and left the library, leaving the house by the side door to avoid the seething hall, on his way to the stables.

❦

"Have you come to see the new colt, sir?" a child's voice piped from somewhere close to where he stood in the stable yard.

"Yes, he's out of Sultana by Atlas, and Judd says we can name him," another voice declared. "Only unofficially, of course, because he has to have a proper stud name."

"Where are you two?" Julius demanded, looking around.

"Here, of course." Two strawberry-blond heads popped up from behind a rain butt. "We're racing water beetles in a bucket."

"You're doing what?" Mystified, he stepped behind the rain butt. "Oh, I see."

The twins had filled a large pail with water in which two water beetles were scudding across the scummy surface, encouraged by little flicks from a desiccated leaf.

"That one's mine," Grace declared, pointing.

"No, it's not, that one's mine," her brother protested. "Mine was always the one on the left."

"No, it isn't, they change sides all the time," Grace stated. "I know mine because he's got one leg shorter than the other."

"Don't be silly, of course he hasn't. Anyway, how do you know it's a he? It could just as easily be a she," Tom pointed out.

"Let's see, then." Grace encouraged one of the creatures onto the leaf, then frowned in puzzlement. "Where do you look? They're not like horses or dogs." She looked up at Julius. "Where do you look, sir?"

"I haven't the faintest idea," he said. "Biology was never my strong suit. Let the poor thing go, now, and show me the colt."

The water beetle and its leaf were dropped into the water, and the two children hurtled off towards the stable block, calling for Judd, who appeared from the stables, hands thrust into the pockets of a baize apron. "Afternoon, m'lord."

"Good afternoon, Judd. Could you have my horse saddled, please?"

"Yes, but you have to see the colt. Doesn't he, Judd? He *has* to see the colt." Grace pranced around Judd.

"All in good time, Grace," Julius said. "You may show me the colt while my horse is being saddled, if that's all right with Judd."

"Oh, aye, sir, 'tis all right by me. Them imps'll show you where he is. But you mind, now," he said, addressing the children. "No shouting, and don't you be gettin' him agitated, or the mare. It'll turn 'er milk."

"I'll make sure they're quiet," Julius said with a quick smile at the groom, who gave a laconic nod before going to fetch the Earl's horse. Julius followed the children into the gloom of the stable block. They led him in exaggerated silence, fingers pressed to lips, to the end of the row, where an elegant chestnut mare was nuzzling a leggy brown colt.

"What should we call him, do you think?" Tom whispered loudly. "We thought Legs because he's all legs, but Judd said he wouldn't always be like that."

"I want to call him Star, because of that little white spot on his head," Grace said in a fierce whisper. "Legs is a silly name."

"Star is boring," her brother objected. "It's ordinary."

"So is Legs."

The mare stirred restlessly, raising her long head to regard her visitors with a somewhat baleful stare. "I think we've overstayed our welcome," Julius said firmly. "Come out, now, and leave them in peace."

The children followed him out into the yard, blinking in the weak sunlight. "Is that your horse? He's so big." Grace gazed up in awe at Julius's raw-boned gray gelding.

"When I'm grown, I'll ride a horse that big," Tom stated. "Nick's Lucifer was that big."

"Lucifer was black," Grace said. "When Nick died, he died." Her tone was matter-of-fact, but Julius could hear a quaver that aroused an unusually powerful emotion in his breast. He had never considered himself in the least sentimental. He couldn't afford to be in his business. He had counted Nick as a friend, one whose death had been inevitable. He had buried him and then turned his face forward to the next step of his mission. What else was there to do?

Just asking himself the question surprised him. He had merely coped as he always had done with such situations, but now he felt a momentary stab of loss and for the first time acknowledged to himself that friends in his world were too few to be easily forgotten.

Judd glanced at both children. Tom had turned away and was idly kicking an upturned barrel, his face averted. The groom looked back at Julius. "Will you mount, my lord?" His voice was crisp, but his eyes were soft and filled with his own sorrow. He held the horse as Julius prepared to swing himself into the saddle.

"That's a fine animal, my lord." Harriet came into the yard, well wrapped in a fur-trimmed cloak, the hood drawn up against the sudden chill of an icy gust of wind. She crossed the cobbles to where he stood by the gelding.

"I can't deny it," the Earl said, running a possessive hand along the curve of the animal's neck.

"What do you call him?" She stroked the velvety nose, and he whickered against her palm.

"Casanova."

"Casanova?" She stared at him incredulously. "What kind of name is that for a horse?"

He smiled. "I've crossed the Bridge of Sighs many times, my dear."

"More times than you've climbed through the casements of wives and maidens?" she queried with raised eyebrows.

"Probably," he returned with the same enigmatic smile. He put a foot in the stirrup and vaulted into the saddle. "If you'll excuse us, Lady Harriet, Casanova needs a good gallop."

She stepped back, opening her palms wide in a gesture of mock permission, and watched him walk the horse out of the yard. He moved as one with his mount in the manner of all superb horsemen. Nick had ridden in the same way, as if he and Lucifer were one whole, with one mind. She blinked rapidly and turned around, remembering her errand.

"Grace . . . Tom, where are you?"

"They're be'ind the rain barrel, my lady," Judd informed her. The children had taken advantage of their sister's momentary distraction to disappear from sight, guessing correctly that they were the object of her arrival in the yard.

She sighed with exasperation and crossed to the barrel. "Come out of there, now. I need you in the house. You'll be expected in the drawing room for tea, and you're both so grubby, it'll take Nurse Maddox an hour to get you respectable again."

"Do we *have* to?" they groaned in chorus.

"Yes," she responded, seizing a hand of each. "The aunts are asking for you."

"Not Great-aunt Augusta," they moaned as she tugged them along beside her.

"Yes, Aunt Augusta and Aunt Sybil are very anxious to see you. And Grandfather will be in the drawing room, too, so you need to be as quiet and civilized as you can possibly manage. Don't forget, tomorrow is Christmas Day."

The reminder silenced further incipient protests, and they trotted along beside her with more equanimity. "The Earl said he doesn't know how to tell the sex of a water beetle," Tom said, as if remembering something of great importance. "Do you know how to tell, Harry?"

The non sequitur startled her into silence for a moment, before she asked mildly, "Why would you be discussing the sex of water beetles with Lord Marbury?"

"Oh, we were racing them, and he came to watch," Grace informed her. "And then we showed him the new colt."

"We like him . . . he's sort of like Nick," Tom said.

"Yes, we like him," Grace concurred. "He's not really like Nick, but he is a little."

Harriet could think of no suitable response to this confidence. Part of her could almost see what they meant. But the man was, of course, a consummate actor. He was a spy, a counterfeit, an assassin, most likely. How could one possibly know his real self, if, indeed, he knew it himself?

Julius gave Casanova his head on the ride into the city, and the horse covered the distance eagerly. Within half an hour, the spires of the city showed against the skyline, and soon they were trotting down the wide thoroughfare of St. Giles, which was thronged on this Christmas Eve with peddlers shouting their wares from the carts they pushed across the cobbles, black-clad members of the University hurrying heads down against the wind, and numerous church bells sounding the hour. Urchins dodged hither and thither, some liberating with quick fingers any trifle, a coin, a purse, or a watch, from unvigilant owners.

Julius turned his horse onto Turl Street, a narrow lane, little more than an alleyway. He rode past Jesus College and drew rein outside a tiny shop on the corner of Market Street. He tethered his horse and went into the dim, musty space that smelled of old documents and dust. A man emerged from the back at the sound of the door. The two men exchanged silent nods of recognition, and Julius climbed a narrow spiral stair at the rear of the shop. It opened into a loft, where the soft rustle of feathers and the sound of cooing pigeons established its purpose.

Julius sat down at a small table in the window and took a slip of paper covered closely in hieroglyphics from his inside pocket. He folded it and inserted it into a tiny capsule, before going to one of the pigeon cages and selecting a bird. The creature came fearlessly to his hand and waited patiently until the little capsule was fastened around its leg. Julius stroked the soft blue-hued neck feathers, murmuring to the bird as he worked. Finally, he went to the window, opening it wide, and set the bird loose with a swift outward motion that enabled it to catch the first updraft of wind. He watched as it rose above the gray walls of the college opposite and then took a decisive turn to the west and disappeared against the late-afternoon sky.

The Earl spent a few more minutes with the birds still in the loft, talking softly to them, caressing their feathers with a long finger stroke, before closing the cages and making his way back down to the shop. He exchanged another wordless nod with the man behind the counter and went back out into the street.

Casanova was pawing the ground, tossing his head impatiently. He didn't like the narrow alley or the constant flow of people past him, and he greeted his master with a whinny. "Very well, my friend, we're on our way." Julius untied the reins. He mounted, settling into the saddle, leaning forward to stroke the horse's neck. "Just one more short stop, and back to a nice warm stable and a bran mash."

The horse stepped out eagerly, and a small child ducked beneath his belly as the quickest route out of his path. "Hey, you, boy." Julius leaned down, seizing the collar of the lad's ragged jerkin. "There's a six-pence for you if you'll run into Jesus, take the first staircase up to the first landing, and knock on the door. Tell the man who answers that Javier is waiting for him in the gatehouse."

The boy stared up at him, caught the glint of silver from the coin Julius held between finger and thumb, nodded, and darted across the street under the arch that led to the college's gatehouse. Julius rode under the arch and waited by the gatehouse.

The college porter stuck his head out of the gate-house, examining his visitor with initial suspicion, but then his expression cleared. "You visitin' again, m'lord?"

"Just for a few moments, Samson. And a Merry Christmas to you." Another silver coin appeared and vanished into the porter's mittened hand.

The man touched his forelock. "Merry Christmas to you, too, m'lord." He disappeared back into the gatehouse.

Julius waited, still mounted, under the arch, looking across the green of the quadrangle, deserted now as the afternoon drew to a close. A few candles showed in the casements that surrounded the quad, and the wind was even brisker, whistling through the archway.

After a few moments, a black-clad figure in the garb of a student emerged from the first staircase, closely followed by the urchin. He gathered his gown around him and hurried to the gatehouse. "M'sieur, we weren't expecting you today." He spoke French in little above a whisper.

"I had a pigeon to fly unexpectedly," Julius said softly in the same language, leaning down from his horse. He tossed the sixpence to the waiting child before saying rapidly, "Tomorrow night, I will have something for you. Come to the rendezvous in the wood at one o'clock. I will mark the tree so you will be certain you're in the right place. The house will be asleep by then, and there will be no danger."

"*Oui, m'sieur. Bien sûr*, I will be there." The French-man turned back to the quad and the staircase from which he'd emerged.

Julius nudged his horse into a walk and rode out into Turl Street. He made one further stop in the city at a small, discreet establishment on Broad Street, then turned Casanova homewards.

He arrived back at Charlbury Hall a little after five. He had ridden Casanova hard, and the horse was ready for his stable, increasing his pace as they turned into the gates of the hall. Julius left him in the hands of a groom, who led him off to the warmth of the stables, and strode back to the house, once again entering through a side door.

The domestic bustle hadn't diminished in his absence, but there was a celebratory air to the house, the smell of logs and candle wax mingling with the rich aromas drifting from the kitchen regions. The great hall was deserted, although it was bright with candles, the yule log burning in the massive fireplace, the scent of pine cones enriching the air. Julius guessed the guests were all in their chambers dressing for the evening, and he took the stairs two at a time to his own apartment.

The lamps were lit, the fire burning bright, the curtains drawn against the encroaching dark. He stood still for a moment, taking the feel of the chamber, before he went to the secretaire, running his fingertips along the narrow drawer beneath the desktop. He felt for the thread that he had inserted half in and half out of the drawer as he'd closed it before he'd left. It wasn't there. The servants would have been in the chamber throughout the day, going about their allotted tasks, but they would have had no business opening the drawer or disturbing anything on the secretaire.

He stood frowning down at the desktop. Maybe it was an accident and he hadn't fixed the thread properly, but if so, it would be the first time in his career. It was a simple test to see if anyone had been nosing about his possessions and one he set every time he left his own chamber, wherever he was. If anyone was spying upon him, the first place they would look would be in his papers and personal possessions.

He sat down and riffled through the scant papers on the secretaire. He had worked late into the previous night, but he had made sure before he slept to burn every piece of paper that he had touched with his quill, even sheets with a mere hint of an indentation on them. Only pristine parchment remained on the desk. Nothing appeared to have been disturbed. And then his gaze sharpened. The inkpot was not exactly where he had left it, perfectly aligned with the quill pen. It had been moved a fraction to one side. Maybe one of the servants had dusted the secretaire that afternoon, but they had put his chamber to rights that morning. Why would it be done twice, particularly with the house in such an uproar and the servants so busy?

Thoughtfully, he pulled the bell rope for Thomas, who appeared in a few minutes with a tray bearing a decanter and a glass. "I thought you'd be glad of a glass of sherry while you dress, my lord." He set the tray on the dresser and went to the armoire.

"A good thought, Thomas. Thank you." Julius shrugged out of his riding coat and unbuttoned his waistcoat. "Have there been any new staff in the house in the last few weeks, Thomas?" He poured himself a glass of sherry and tugged at the knot in his cravat.

"Not as far as I know, m'lord." Thomas held up a dark gray silk coat. "Will you wear this tonight, sir, with the dove-gray britches?"

"If you think so," his lordship said with a faintly dismissive gesture, pulling his shirt over his head. "No new staff were hired to help out over Christmas?"

"No, m'lord. Just a couple of girls from the village to give a 'and in the kitchen and the still room, but they always comes up when a few extra's needed. Just local folk, everyone knows everyone around 'ere." The manservant laid a gray-striped waistcoat reverently on the bed and turned to the linen press for stockings. "Most of us folks 'ave worked up at the 'all since we was nippers."

"So, no newcomers in the last months, then?" Julius repeated in a musing tone.

"No, m'lord." Thomas handed his lordship the white knit stockings.

Julius dressed with only half his mind on the task. Fortunately, Thomas knew what he was about, and within half an hour, the manservant stood back to admire his creation, brushing an imaginary speck from the perfectly fitting shoulder of the gray silk coat. "Any jewelry, my lord . . . a stud or pin, perhaps, for the cravat?"

Julius opened a small box on the dresser and took out a jet stud, fixing it into the snowy folds of his cravat.

"Perfect, if I might say so, m'lord." Thomas nodded his approval. "Just the right understated touch with the gray."

"I'm delighted you think so, Thomas." Julius dropped an ebony snuffbox into his coat pocket and walked to the door. "I think I hear the carolers."

"Indeed, my lord." Thomas went to the window, pulling aside the curtain. "They're coming up the drive now."

Julius made his leisurely way down to the great hall, where the guests were congregating around the fire. The Duke stood with his back to the blaze, a resplendent if somewhat old-fashioned figure in a gold damask coat and matching britches, an emerald ring flashing on his finger and a similarly lustrous pin throwing green fire from the extravagant fall of Mechlin lace at his throat.

"Ah, Marbury, dear boy, come and meet m'sisters," he called as Julius reached the bottom step.

Julius obliged, making his bow deeply to the Ladies Augusta and Sybil. He couldn't see Harriet anywhere in the group, but the Duke introduced him around the circle. The singing from without grew louder and had just reached a crescendo outside the double front doors when Harriet came down the stairs, a child, a remarkably scrubbed and tidy child, in each hand.

"Open the door," she instructed them in a quick whisper. They scampered across the expanse of oak floor and, with the surreptitious aid of a footman, hauled open the great doors. The carolers, sconced torches held high, stepped into the hall. "God Rest Ye

Merry Gentlemen" rang to the rafters. When the final note died, the children darted forward with plates of mince pies and marzipan, offering them among the singers, whom the servants plied with steaming mugs of mulled wine.

The Duke came forward to greet the singers, all of whom, Julius noticed, he knew by name, and after shaking hands all around, he presented the leader of the group with a purse. A final burst of song, and the carolers went back into the cold Christmas Eve. The doors were closed, and a buzz of conversation arose among the guests around the fireplace.

Harriet came up to the Earl. "So, my lord, did you enjoy your ride this afternoon?"

"Very much, I thank you." He accepted a glass of sherry from a circulating footman. "I'm assuming your afternoon was spent rather tediously." He watched her expression, his eyes narrowed a little. But there was not the slightest flicker of unease in those luminous green eyes.

"If you mean ensuring that the bedchambers had been allotted aright, with a plentiful supply of mustard baths, sal volatile, and hip baths for those who insist upon them, you would be right, sir." She sipped from her own glass. "Not to mention trying to keep the twins out of trouble."

He smiled sympathetically, reflecting that with such a catalogue of tasks, Lady Harriet couldn't possibly have found time to comb through his bedchamber. And why would she, anyway? He knew she had acted as Nick's poste restante during his and Nick's mission to France, but her brother had never implied that she had any more active a part. And there was no way Harriet could know that he himself had been with Nick on that mission. Even under duress, Nick would have never broken protocol by revealing his colleague's identity. Harriet herself had said that her brother had never mentioned Julius Forsythe to her. And there was no one else to do so.

And yet . . . and yet, who else?

There were no new servants, no possible intelligence agents among this Society house party. There was only Nick's sister.

And she was looking utterly radiant, he thought, despite her tedious afternoon. Her gown of bronze silk clung to her figure in a most enticing fashion. It was caught high under her breasts, where nestled a topaz pendant. She wore topaz ear drops, and in her hair was a silver fillet studded with the same stones. Her eyes glinted green and gold in the lamplight, and her hair shone like corn silk under the sun.

What was the matter with him? He never noticed women in any detail; he didn't have time. And he couldn't afford the distraction; it could mean his life. Not here, though, surely, he amended, looking around the room, noting the smiling, self-satisfied faces, the festive air, the lively bubble of voices. What harm would it do if he indulged in a little dalliance with this alluring creature? He'd have to be blind not to appreciate her charms, and an insensate idiot not to respond to them.

But someone had been in his possessions that afternoon.

Chapter Six

"My dear, I trust you've arranged for Marbury to take you into dinner?" The Duke approached his grand-daughter through the guests still gathered around the fireplace.

"If that is what you wish, sir," Harriet responded, her smile giving nothing away. "I had thought per-haps the courtesy was owed Lord Delford. He is a first cousin, after all."

"And as such, family," her grandfather declared, tossing off the contents of his wine glass with an air of finality. "Family come second when there are other guests. It would please me if you took personal care of Marbury. I find him congenial company, and I've no wish to force him to endure the inanities of some of the party . . . who shall remain nameless," he added with a baleful stare at his sister Augusta.

He didn't lower his voice, and Harriet winced a little, glancing quickly around, but in the general buzz of conversation, it seemed the remark had gone unnoticed. "You'll take Dowager Lady Belling in."

"For my sins," he agreed. "She will go on about that husband of hers. Died at least ten years ago, and a debauched fool into the bargain, but she still seems to think he sits at God's right hand."

Harriet suppressed a smile. It was all too accurate a description of the late Lord Belling. "His grace of Harwich will take Aunt Augusta. They like each other and should enjoy themselves."

The Duke nodded his approval. "And send Delford in with Hartford's daughter. She's a pretty little thing, although something of a mouse, but I daresay he won't mind that."

Harriet curtsied her acknowledgment of these instructions. She knew well her grandfather's general view of his relatives. His tolerance seemed to extend only to his late son and his grandchildren, and even that could be somewhat edgy at times. She looked across the room to where Julius stood gallantly conversing with the great-aunts, who were ensconced side-by-side on a cushioned settle to one side of the hearth, glasses of ratafia in hand, lorgnettes resting on pouter-pigeon bosoms.

There could be no possible attraction for the Earl in such an unfashionable Christmas house party. There were few prominent members of Society gathered at Charlbury Hall. Most of the men were members of the House of Lords, but as far as she knew, none of them was particularly active in politics. The younger members of the party all seemed barely out of school compared with the Earl's composed assurance. He was older than Nick, she was sure. Although Nick, too, had carried himself with the same poise and gravitas. So why had the man chosen to spend the Christmas season there of all places?

There was only the one obvious explanation . . . the one provided by the men from the Ministry. Julius Forsythe was engaged in clandestine activity with the network of foreign spies who they knew were working out of Oxford University. Charlbury Hall was ideally situated, less than ten miles from the dreaming spires. And if it was true that the Earl was using Nick's family as cover for his betrayal of his country, then it was a double betrayal of Nick.

For a moment, Harriet was swamped with a red

surge of fury and grief so powerful she felt sick and dizzy, the room around her fading into a gray mist so that she wondered if she was about to faint. But then, abruptly, she became aware that the object of her fury was looking at her, eyebrows raised in question. She realized that she had been staring fixedly at him, and she could only imagine her expression if it had been an accurate reflection of her thoughts. She felt her cheeks warm and with a supreme effort produced a smile, acknowledging his gaze, and then watched with sinking heart as, with a murmur of apology to the aunts, he threaded his way deftly towards her.

"I have the impression you wished to talk to me, Lady Harriet," he said, bowing before her. "How may I be of service?"

"Forgive me," she said with a tiny laugh. "I didn't realize I was staring at you. The Duke has just given me instructions as to the seating plan this evening, and it's thrown all my carefully thought-out decisions to the four winds. I was racking my brains trying to rearrange things."

"Oh, well, that's something of a relief," he said. "Your expression implied that you were slowly roasting someone over hot coals . . . or at least wishing you were. I felt quite sorry for whoever it was." His tone was teasing, his smile relaxed and easy.

Harriet regained her composure. "In some measure, it was you, my lord." She gave a light laugh. "As it happens, the Duke wishes you to take me into dinner, and it was that change that was causing me so much annoyance."

He wrinkled his nose comically. "Annoyance . . . well, that has certainly put me in my place."

"No, indeed, sir, I did not mean such discourtesy. It was only the consequences of the instruction that were inconvenient. I shall be delighted to have your company at dinner." Harriet was astonished at herself. She had never really considered herself much of an actress, but she thought she sounded utterly convincing; even her laughter sounded genuine.

Julius bowed again. "The pleasure will be all mine, ma'am." He took her empty glass and exchanged it for a full one from the tray of a passing footman. "But if we are to be dinner partners, could we not dispense with formality, Harriet? I asked you this morning if you would call me by my given name. It would please me greatly."

"Maybe it would, sir, but it would certainly draw

adverse attention from my aunts," she retorted, taking a sip of wine. "They are great sticklers for the conventions, you should understand."

"Then when we are private, perhaps?" he persevered.

"I doubt there will be much opportunity for that, Lord Marbury. I have many guests to attend to."

"You really are determined to be obstructive, aren't you?" he observed. "Oddly enough, Nick never mentioned that particular quirk of yours."

"You were in the habit of discussing me with my brother, then, sir?" Her tone acquired a degree of hauteur, and she was aware that she was hurt as much as anything by the idea that Nick would discuss her with this man but not tell her anything about the Earl in exchange. What had they had together that was so exclusive, Nicholas Devere and Julius Forsythe?

"My dear Harriet, he spoke of you only in the most fond manner. You were much in his thoughts, I gathered. You and the twins. I had the impression he hated to leave you alone."

He spoke quietly, and the black eyes had taken on a texture almost like black velvet, Harriet thought. He was doing it again, enclosing them both in some exclusive circle, where nothing around them could penetrate. She took an overlarge sip of her wine and turned her head, coughing into her hand, shattering the uncomfortably private moment.

The brass gong provided welcome diversion. Mallow, the butler, stood at the foot of the staircase and announced, "Dinner is served, your grace."

The Duke bowed to the Dowager Lady Belling, offering his arm. Harriet swiftly paired the remaining guests with a smile, a nod, a hand on an arm, and took up the rear of the procession on the arm of Lord Marbury. The dining salon was brilliantly lit. Chandeliers threw torchlight onto the shining rosewood surface of the immense table, and candelabra marched, silver-bright, down the center. A fire burned in the massive inglenook fireplace, dispelling the chill in the air, heavy curtains were drawn across the long windows, effectively blocking drafts, and hidden from view beneath the table, small warming pans of hot coals dispensed heat to frozen feet.

Julius held Harriet's chair for her as she took her place at the center of the right side of the table, and then he took his own seat on her right. Aunt Augusta presided at the foot of the table, the Duke at the head.

"The children are not making an appearance at the

dinner table, I gather," Julius observed, taking up his soupspoon.

"No, but they will tomorrow. We will dine at four tomorrow, so that the servants may have their own Christmas dinner in the evening." Harriet took a spoonful of chestnut soup. "I am surprised, sir, that you are not spending Christmas with your own family. You mentioned a sister and children, as I recall." She broke off a piece of bread and glanced sideways at him. "Christmas is usually a time to be with one's family, not a party of strangers."

"I don't consider the Duke a stranger," he responded. "This is excellent soup, by the way . . . And neither do I consider you to be a stranger, if I may say so without impertinence. Your brother talked so often of you."

"You are a stranger to me, Lord Marbury." She glanced at him again. "I had never heard of you before yesterday afternoon."

"No," he agreed blandly. "As I've said, your brother must have considered my friendship to be less noteworthy than I considered his."

"I don't believe that," she said directly, deciding she would get nowhere by continuing to tiptoe around the subject. "Nick was always very loyal to his friends, and he and I had few secrets from each other. There must have been some compelling reason for him to keep *you* a secret."

"I can't think of one," he responded. "And since we are unlikely to discover the answer now, maybe we should stop worrying about it."

Harriet tried another tack. "Were you with Nick at the siege of Elba when he was killed?"

He shook his head. "No, I was never in the army."

And neither was Nick, she reflected. Or at least, not in the regular army. "So you were just companions in pleasure, then?" She took a slice of roast turbot from the platter presented by a footman.

"That is certainly one way of putting it." He helped himself liberally to fish.

She took a delicate forkful. "The turbot is one of Cook's specialties, by the way. She uses ginger and cinnamon in the sauce. I hope you like it."

"It's quite delicious."

"Did you spend time together in London, or just in Paris and here at Charlbury?"

Julius put down his fork and turned to look at her quizzically. "This is quite a catechism, ma'am."

"Given how close I was to my brother, curiosity about how he spent his time away from his family seems only natural in the circumstances."

"I suppose so." He picked up his fork again, and Harriet waited for him to answer her question, but he seemed intent on his turbot.

She waited until the fish was removed and roast goose made its appearance, then repeated her question. "So, did you see much of Nick in London?" She forked a slice of meat from the silver platter presented by a footman.

"Not really." He selected a plump, crisp-skinned leg.

Harriet took a spoonful of greens cooked in almond milk from the tureen at her elbow. "You were such friends, I wonder why that should be . . . Do you care for applesauce?"

"Thank you." He took the bowl from her. "Let me explain. I remained in Paris when Nick returned to England." He gave her a bland smile. "Since I understand you spend most of your time in London yourself, I'm sure, since you shared a roof with your brother, you would have been aware of our friendship had I been in London."

It was like trying to shoot a mosquito, Harriet thought in frustration. He managed to evade every single question while appearing to answer her openly.

"How often were you with Nick down here at Charlbury?" She tried again.

"Oh, several times . . . I don't recall exactly. But you should talk to your grandfather. Maybe he remembers better than I."

"Maybe." She gave him a brief smile and turned to engage her neighbor on her left side, leaving the Earl to do the same with his own.

Once the detritus of the goose had been removed and replaced with mushroom tartlets, scalloped oysters, and some cheese and parsnip fritters, Harriet turned back to Julius. "Your sister . . . ?" she prompted. "How many children has she?"

"Three or four," he returned, taking a sip of wine.

"You don't know exactly?" she exclaimed. "But you gave me the impression you were very fond of them."

"Oh, so I am," he agreed. "When in their company. But that doesn't mean I can always keep track of how many there are. Eloise is usually either with child or just delivered of one." He dabbed at his mouth with his napkin and gave her a sideways smile. "Her husband is very devoted, it seems." It was a wickedly suggestive smile that brought an instant and involuntary smile to her lips, although she was sure the aunts would have expected a maidenly blush.

"Is she your only sister?"

"Yes . . . and to save your next question, I am now her only brother. Our older brother died of smallpox when he was twelve." His smile now was quizzical, slightly teasing. "Perhaps a written questionnaire would move matters along a little."

"Oh, don't be absurd," Harriet declared. "I am merely trying to make conversation."

"Well, if I may say so, interrogation is an unusual form of conversation." He spooned scalloped oysters onto his plate. "I must congratulate you on your cook. Has she been with the family long?"

Harriet laughed. "Oh, very well, sir. I yield the floor. Yes, Mistress Hubbard has been cook at Charlbury since before my grandmother died. She and Mallow were here before Nick was born and were part of our childhood, as they are part of the twins'. The same with Judd." She switched onto a parallel track. "Where did you go on your ride today? I should have told you about some of my favorite rides around here. The countryside is so beautiful, even in the middle of winter."

"I certainly found it so," Julius responded. "But as it happens, I decided to ride into Oxford. I was a student there many years ago and always enjoyed the weeks before Christmas, when the city took on such a festive air. I had the urge to see how much it had changed in the last ten years."

"And had it?"

"Probably not, but I have," he said with a chuckle. "For some reason, the scents of roasting chestnuts from the braziers along St. Giles or the spice cakes they were selling in Carfax didn't have the same richness as they did when I was a gangling and perpetually famished undergraduate."

"You make yourself sound like a world-weary old man," Harriet scoffed. "You cannot be that much older than Nick, and he never lost his pleasure in the city at any time of the year."

Julius looked at her rather more sharply. "I can give Nick eight years, my dear. And you, nine."

That would make him thirty. Harriet had thought him about that age, although his manner sometimes made him seem older. She observed, "Eight years is quite an age difference when it comes to friendship. It seems unusual that you and Nick should have been as close as you imply just based on pleasures shared. A joint enterprise perhaps might forge strong ties that could transcend such a gap, but just cards, or sportsmanship, or dancing . . . come to think of it, Nick was never much of a dancer." She regarded him with an air of mild inquiry. "What did you have in common, my lord?"

Julius considered his response. The lady was fishing, and she was fishing in quite good waters. She had acted as Nick's poste restante, so she knew at least something of Nick's extracurricular activities, and she was no fool. Her questions as a result were pertinent. But should he satisfy her curiosity with a fraction of the truth or continue in straight-faced denial?

The latter would probably close off all possibility of getting to know her better. That had not been an object of this particular Christmas excursion, but it was one that seemed to have become very important. He liked her. No, much more than that. She attracted him most powerfully. Not just physically, although he'd be the last to deny that particular attraction, but he enjoyed her company, and he admired her. And for Julius, admiration was the most powerful aphrodisiac. She had so much courage, and she was carrying far too much on those slender shoulders. He wanted to lighten her burdens a little. She had shared them with Nick, and her brother was no longer there to take his part. Nick had made his own choices, chosen the path that had led to his early death. But others had

been complicit in that tragedy, too. With the smooth-
ness of a greased wheel, his mind automatically threw
up the wall that prevented further exploration of that
subject. What was done was done.

But Harriet was too young to carry the weight of so
much loss, not to mention the responsibility for the
twins. Of course, legally they were their grandfather's
charge, but it was as clear as day to Julius that their
day-to-day care, both emotional and physical, fell to
their sister. And that didn't seem right to him. Nick
had said as much on several occasions, and Julius now
understood what he meant, now that he had met
Nick's beloved sister. There was no real reason he
should create a rift between them at this juncture.

"There was an incident while we were in Paris.
I'm surprised your brother didn't tell you of it, but
perhaps he didn't wish to alarm you," he said with
a slight shrug, accepting a refilled glass from a footman with a decanter. "We were involved in a street
fight—"

"A street fight?" Harriet interrupted him. "A
brawl?"

"Not exactly," Julius said, considering his words.
"I came upon a young man being set upon by a trio
of bully boys, and since the odds struck me as some-

what uneven, I took my sword to the fight. I was hard pressed at one point, and by great good fortune, Nick happened to come around the corner and jumped in at the opportune moment. I think it no exaggeration to say that both my life and that of the young man were saved by his timely intervention."

"Oh, I see." Harriet absorbed this. She could believe such a story of Nick. But what if Julius had actually been one of the assassins and not an angel of mercy, and Nick had assumed that someone was in trouble and joined the fight without knowing anything about the participants or the cause of the imbroglio? But then again, Julius, as a double agent, could have been set upon by British assassins and Nick had happened to come to his rescue without knowing that he was helping the wrong man. Oh, it gave her a headache. Nothing was to be gained by such pointless speculation.

"That would certainly explain an unlikely friendship," she said easily. "Nick was ever one to go to the rescue of the underdog." She wondered with a degree of mischief whether the term *underdog* had bruised his lordship's pride somewhat. But if it had, he gave no indication.

"Your aunt appears to be signaling you," Julius

murmured, bringing her attention back to the table.

Harriet looked towards her aunt and saw her gesticulating with her eyebrows. Augusta was far too well-bred to call down the table to gain her great-niece's attention. Harriet inclined her head in acknowledgment and made a move to rise from her chair. The signal was sufficient for the gentlemen to rise to assist the ladies from their chairs, and Aunt Augusta led the female procession from the dining room.

Before going into the drawing room, Harriet ran upstairs to the nursery floor. The nursemaid was sitting in front of the fire, darning Tom's stockings, but she jumped up as Harriet came in. "No, please, sit down, Lilly. Has Nurse Maddox gone to bed?"

"Yes, m'lady. She said she'll be up early enough wi' the children in the morning, so she went early."

"She's right," Harriet said with a rueful smile. "They'll be up before dawn on Christmas morning. Are they asleep now?" She gestured to the door to the night nursery.

The girl nodded. "I looked in on 'em just a few minutes ago, m'lady. They're out like lights."

"Good . . . then you go to your bed, too, Lilly." Harriet went to a cupboard and took a box from the top shelf. "Sugar plums have always been a tradition on Christmas morning when the children wake early, so make sure they get these. I know Nurse Maddox will grumble, she always does, but she doesn't really object. They may come down to me at eight o'clock but not before. I daresay I shall be late abed tonight."

"Yes, indeed, m'lady." Lilly was putting away her darning. She took the wooden box from Harriet and set it on the dresser.

"Good night, then." Harriet left the nursery and returned downstairs to take her place in the drawing room while the ladies awaited the men.

Julius was one of the first men to leave the dining room. He looked around the elegant salon, where women sat in little groups, holding cups of tea and chattering among themselves. Only Harriet stood alone in front of a window. She was holding the heavy curtain aside, looking out into the dark. He came up behind her and laid a hand on the soft rounded curve of a sloping shoulder. The bare skin was warm beneath his fingers.

She jumped, turned her head, her green eyes wide. "You startled me, sir."

"Forgive me." He kept his hand where it was, cupping the curve of her shoulder. "You seemed so absorbed. I was wondering what you could see out there in the cold dark." His voice was soft, and she could feel his breath warm against her ear.

That feeling of intimacy came over her again, enclosing them in their own space while the hushed murmurs of the salon faded into the distance. "I was looking for snowflakes," she responded as softly. "Remembering the magic of a white Christmas in my own childhood. The children would be ecstatic, although Grandfather would be devastated." She turned with a little laugh, shrugging slightly so that his hand fell from her shoulder. "Divided loyalties, as always. Don't you find them the very devil, my lord?"

"A personal question which I will answer if it's asked in a personal fashion," he responded with a smile that brought the deep lustre to his black eyes. "My name will supply an answer, Harriet."

"Do you not find divided loyalties to be the very devil, Julius?" she asked, holding his gaze.

"I do what I can to avoid them," he answered her. His hand moved, for an instant touched the curve of her cheek, and then fell to his side. "But yes, when they cannot be avoided, they are indeed devil's spawn."

A moment of silence fell between them. It was not an awkward silence, but it held something, a portent, a promise, a world of things unsaid.

Then he said lightly, "So what does the morning hold for us, my lady hostess?"

"Well, since none of our company is fit to go to midnight mass, having all eaten and drunk their fill this evening, matins will be an obligatory event," she replied in like manner. "We shall process after breakfast at ten-thirty or thereabouts. The church, as you know, is just beyond the gates, so it's a short walk. After that, there will be a party of sorts here in the great hall for the tenants and the folk from the village. You need not be there, but the family must, of course. Dinner will be at four."

"And is there a gift exchange?"

"No, but Grandfather, myself, and the children have a small ceremony before breakfast." She smiled. "They will be up at the crack of dawn."

He nodded. "Then may I suggest you take yourself to bed now? You have performed your hostess duties admirably, and I can see not the slightest reason you should not slip away to the peace and privacy of your own bedchamber. You are looking sadly fatigued, dear girl." A fingertip brushed the skin beneath her eyes. "Nick always said you took on too much."

"I know he did." For a treacherous instant, Harriet felt as if she could lean into this man, take some of his strength for herself, as she had done with her brother. But Julius Forsythe was a suspected double agent, an assassin. Her task was to prove this. She couldn't do that from the protection of his arms.

She stepped away from him, her smile suddenly brittle. "I will take your advice, sir. Thank you. Good night." She moved away across the room, pausing for a moment beside her aunt before disappearing through the double doors.

Now, what the hell happened to change her mood so suddenly? Julius stood frowning, before he, too, slipped from the room to the solitude of his own chamber.

Chapter Seven

Thomas was laying out his lordship's nightgown when Julius entered his bedchamber. "A nice evening, m'lord?" He smoothed down the coverlet.

"Very pleasant, thank you, Thomas. I shan't need you any more today."

"You don't need me to help you undress, m'lord?" Thomas sounded a little put out.

Julius shook his head, loosening his cravat with one hand. "No, I'm more than capable of putting myself to bed. You may wake me in the morning at eight o'clock."

"If you're sure, m'lord. I trust everything is to your satisfaction. Mr. Mallow will want to know, sir."

"You may tell him that everything is very much to

my satisfaction," Julius reassured him. "Now, go and enjoy the rest of your evening."

"Very well, m'lord. There is cognac in the decanter on the dresser should you wish for a nightcap." Thomas bowed and left.

Julius shook his head. He was so accustomed to looking after himself most of the time that the constant presence of servants could at times be quite oppressive. But when in Rome . . .

He shrugged out of his coat and poured himself a goblet of cognac, carrying the glass to the window, where he drew back the heavy velvet curtain. The sweep of lawn at the front of the house was partially illuminated by the pitch torches that blazed on either side of the double front doors. The rest of the garden was in shadow, although a fitful moon occasionally skipped out from behind heavy cloud cover. The woods that surrounded the lawn formed a solid black shape, but Julius knew that they were not as dense as they appeared to be and that within them were several small clearings. In one of them, he would meet Marcel the following night.

He sipped his cognac, frowning. His contact had precise instructions as to how to find the rendezvous, but as there were several clearings, he had told Marcel he would find a mark on a tree in the correct place. He had intended to leave the marker in the clearing at some point during the day tomorrow, but now he wondered if he might find it difficult to slip away alone and undetected on Christmas Day itself. Better to do it now, when there was no possibility of anyone seeing him.

He set down his glass and took a thick cloak from the armoire. He had spent enough time at Charlbury Hall to know his way down the backstairs and met no one as he descended. He let himself out through a side door and walked briskly along the gravel path around the side of the house and out onto the lawn. A thick frost was already forming, and the grass crunched beneath his booted feet. He kept to the side of the lawn, in the shadow of the woods, until he reached the opening that gave onto a wide alley that led through the trees.

Harriet stood at her own bedchamber window, staring at the shape moving along the shadowy edge of the woods. Who could it be? Who would be wandering around the garden at midnight on Christmas Eve?

But she knew. There was something so familiar

about the way the figure moved, a fluid, easy grace, a swing from the hip, a firm, crisp step. Why was Julius Forsythe roaming around the grounds on a freezing night?

It was her job to find out.

Without a second thought, Harriet wrapped herself tightly in her fur-lined cloak and flew down the stairs and out of the front door. She had no reason to hide the fact that she was taking a short stroll before bed, however eccentric it might seem. It was her family house, and she was her own mistress, free to do as she pleased.

She darted to the side of the lawn, following the imprint of booted feet in the frost. They led into the darkness of the wood, and she hesitated for a moment. Although she knew the woods like the back of her hand, there was something intimidating about stepping into that dark void. She couldn't see the Earl's footsteps amidst the trees and stood very still, listening, straining her ears to catch the slightest sound. A twig broke somewhere ahead of her, and she jumped, her nostrils flaring in the icy air. What was he doing? Was he meeting someone? She took a tentative step forward, moving into the darkness, then stopped to listen again.

Then she heard it. The sound of a footstep just ahead of her on the path, and it was coming towards her. Her heart leaped into her throat as she jumped sideways off the path and behind the thick trunk of an ancient oak. Julius materialized out of the darkness, a shapeless form wrapped tightly in a cloak, and Harriet held her breath, praying he would walk past her and out through the trees onto the lawn without stopping.

But he did stop. Just short of the oak tree. He stopped and stood motionless, listening. Then, slowly, he turned his head and looked behind him. Something had attracted his attention.

If he discovered her, she'd have to have some logical, rational explanation. Harriet desperately tried to think of some reason she would be out there in the freezing midnight darkness. And then the Earl took a step again, continuing on his way down the alley and out onto the lawn.

Harriet breathed again but stayed where she was, clinging to the tree trunk, utterly still for as long as she could bear. At last, when she was sure he had to have reached the house, she slipped out from the protection of the tree and crept to the edge of the wood. Hiding behind a holly bush vivid and bursting with bright red berries, she peered out onto the lawn. It was deserted. As she stood there, the front doors opened, and a servant emerged from the brightly lit hall and doused the pitch torches, plunging the entire garden into blackness. A few candles burned in some of the upper chambers, but one by one, the reception rooms became dark, and she was alone in the night.

Her eyes had accustomed themselves to the darkness, and the clouds were not so thick, offering a weak light from both moon and stars. She turned back into the woods. The wide alley between the trees stretched ahead into darkness, but she was confident now that she could find her way without mishap. What was she looking for? The Earl had been in the woods for a very short time, so he couldn't have gone too far. He hadn't been gone long enough to meet someone, she was sure of it. So what had he done?

She began to walk slowly down the alley, looking to right and left for any sign of disturbance, any flattening of the grass that would indicate someone had passed by or a recently broken twig on a bush. The path opened into a wide clearing where the moonlight was sufficient to give reasonable visibility. Harriet walked slowly around the space, looking for something. If only she knew what. She could see nothing out of the ordinary and was beginning to feel cold despite the fur cloak. She was also very tired. It had been a long day, and the morrow promised to be no less active. But something kept her from giving up too easily. She had only come a very short way into the woods.

She veered onto a side path to the right of the clearing. It was narrower and darker, but she followed it until it, too, opened into a clearing, a much smaller one this time. She stood looking around for a moment, remembering how she and Nick had loved this spot in the summer, when the sun threw dappled light down through the overhanging copper beeches. In the center was a small spring bubbling up from the ground, which they assumed was somehow connected to the River Cherwell, which flowed along the edge of the estate. Maybe the source of an underground stream.

She traversed the clearing rapidly, and then something on the slender trunk of a silver birch caught her eye. A bright white mark stood out against the pale bark. She went close, peering at it. It was a hieroglyphic of some kind that reminded her of the impress of markings she had seen on the Earl's secretaire. She peered closely at it. It was not carved into the bark but chalked onto it. A message for someone? A temporary message for someone who would be looking for it. The chalk would wash away in the first heavy rain, so Julius expected it to be found soon.

But her work was done for the night. She had no idea what the marking meant and not a hope of discovering its meaning, at least not that night. But she could find plenty of excuses to visit the clearing, the twins would always happily accompany her, and she would keep a watchful eye on the space over the next few days. Maybe someone would leave an answering mark.

They would have locked all of the outside doors, but she and Nick had always kept a spare key to the kitchen hidden in the henhouse. They had often crept out of the house at night when they were children to watch a badger's set in the woods. When the babies had come out to play in the moonlight, the children had watched for hours, fascinated and entranced by their gamboling. She and Nick had intended to take the twins on their first midnight foray on their eleventh birthday. But then Nick had died. And Harriet didn't know whether she'd feel like doing it alone.

Gathering the thick folds of her cloak around her, she hurried for the house, taking the side path that took her into the kitchen garden. She opened the henhouse door, feeling for the key on the little ledge above. The hens stirred restlessly, fearing a fox, as her fingers closed over the brass key. She murmured a word of reassurance and backed out, closing the door and dropping the heavy bar across it.

The kitchen was lit only by the glow of the range, but it gave Harriet sufficient light to fetch milk from the pantry and fill a copper pan, which she set on the hob. She realized that she was feeling a bit shaky after her excursion, although at the time she'd thought herself perfectly calm. The automatic business of heating milk and warming her frozen hands at the range restored her equilibrium. She poured her milk into a china beaker and made her way up to her own quarters.

She poured a little brandy into her milk and sat by the fire, warming her feet, sipping her drink, and puzzling over the significance of the Earl's marking. It had to be a sign of some kind, intended for someone to see. But who? A French agent? Any way you looked at it, it was certainly suspicious behavior for a man ostensibly enjoying a Christmas house party in the Oxfordshire countryside, and it would give her something substantial to pass along to the men at the Ministry even if she discovered nothing else.

All in all, a satisfactory evening's work, she decided

when she finally curled up in her feather mattress under the feather quilt and snuffed out the candle. But somehow she didn't feel as pleased as she thought she should, and as she lay wakeful, watching the flicker of firelight against the wall, she realized that she had no wish to discover that Julius Forsythe was a French double agent. No wish at all.

Julius sat by his own fireside, sipping cognac and considering the situation. Someone had been out there with him. He had completed his task, leaving the chalk mark on the tree for Marcel to discover on the morrow, and as he was making his way back through the trees, he had realized that he was not alone.

It was a sixth sense, that sense of danger, bred into him after years in the service, and he knew never to contradict it. He had heard nothing, seen nothing, and yet that other presence had been as obvious to him as if whoever it was had shouted out loud.

Of course, he could have looked, and probably would have found the person, but that would have been too simple. If there was a plot afoot, he would prefer to let it develop. And if it was nothing, then that would become clear enough.

He leaned back in his chair, closing his eyes. It was, of course, always possible that Harriet had been following him. If it was she who had been going through his possessions that afternoon, it would be no stretch of the imagination to assume that if she had caught sight of him in the garden, she might have taken it into her rather beautiful head to follow him. The only truly puzzling question was why she was spying on him in the first place. Did she know something? Despite her denial, *had* Nick told her something of his association with Julius? Was she following some whim or curiosity of her own, or did she have a real reason to suspect him of something?

Not that it mattered in the least. A slight cynical smile touched his lips. Lovely though she was, intelligent and courageous though she undoubtedly was, Lady Harriet Devere was no match for him in the spying game. But maybe it could play to his hand to let her think she was for a while. He'd already admitted to himself how much he wanted to cultivate her. The deeper their attraction to each other grew, the more likely it was that he'd discover what she was up to, what it was that she knew, or thought she knew.

It was all business, he told himself. False pretenses were his stock in trade. Harriet was up to her own game, so why shouldn't he play his? *But why does the idea leave such an unpleasant taste in my mouth?*

Nick would not object. In fact, a liaison of sorts between his dearest friend and his beloved sister would probably please him. He had sometimes hinted at such a thing, talking of arranging a weekend at Charlbury after their mission, where Harry and Julius could meet each other at last.

Such damnable luck had haunted them on that dreadful afternoon in Bruges.

He reached for the decanter, his gaze suddenly blank as his mind went back to the moments that had ended the life of Nicholas, Viscount Hesketh. It was a memory he avoided when he could, but tonight it would not be repressed.

The narrow cobbled streets of Bruges were bathed in late-afternoon sun when Nick and Julius emerged from a corner tavern. They were alone, their drinking companions still quaffing tankards of ale in boisterous camaraderie. Nick had commented that he felt a little woozy. Julius had laughed, chiding him for drinking too much, to which Nick had protested that he never allowed himself to get foxed and certainly not on a mission. All of which was true, Julius had agreed. He had watched Nick closely, waiting for the moment when the sleeping draught took sufficient effect for Nick to declare himself ready to return to their room at the Coq d'Or. It would knock him out for at least six hours, time enough for Julius to accomplish his own mission. The moment came finally when Nick swayed and grabbed onto the jamb of a door that stood open to the afternoon's warmth. "Don't know what's come over me, dear fellow, but I need m'bed," he slurred. "I'll go back to the inn. No need to come with me."

Julius had calculated quickly. The inn was around the next corner, and he judged Nick capable of reaching there unaided. He had his own business to attend to. He glanced up the narrow lane. It was for the moment deserted. "Are you sure you don't want me to escort you?"

"Absolutely, m'dear fellow. I'll be at the inn in a moment." Nick passed his hand across his brow and swayed a little. "Good God, I think I must be coming down with a fever."

"I'll only be an hour, and then, if you're still unwell, I'll fetch the apothecary," Julius said. "But I think 'tis just the strong ale, my friend. It can catch one unawares."

Nick looked doubtful. He shook his head as if he could dispel the dizziness. Then he lurched off around the corner. Julius turned in the opposite direction, and as he did so, he heard the shout, the clash of blades. He ran *to the corner and watched in helpless immobility as two men with short swords attacked Nicholas, who put up a gallant defense. If he had not been addled with the sleeping draught, he would have dispatched both men easily enough, but in his present condition, he was no match for one of them, let alone both. Nick slipped in his own blood to the cobbles in front of the inn, and Julius swiftly melted into the shadows of an adjoining alley. He knew who had sent the two men, and they would be looking for him next. He had his own life to preserve and his own mission to accomplish.*

An acknowledgment that brought him no more comfort now than it had done then. What had Harriet said that evening? Something about divided loyalties, how they were the very devil. Well, she had never spoken a truer word, and he was resigned to a lifetime of guilt and grief over the choice he had made that afternoon in Bruges.

Chapter Eight

Christmas morning dawned bright and crisp, sun glinting off frost-rimed lawns. Harriet was awakened when the children leaped upon her bed with cries of "Merry Christmas, Harry! We got sugar plums!"

She blinked blearily at the two glowing faces. "So I can see," she murmured. "You've both got sugar moustaches, and your hands are all sticky." She pulled herself up in the bed and squinted at the ormolu clock on the mantel. "Merry Christmas . . . but you're half an hour early. I said eight o'clock." She was smiling as she said it, and the children were not fooled.

"We couldn't wait a moment longer to wish you Merry Christmas," Grace said. "We've been to the kitchen and wished everyone there a Merry Christmas."

"And for our breakfast, Mistress Hubbard gave us two of the marzipan sheep from the nativity scene she made out of ginger cake and icing for the servants' Christmas dinner tonight. And Mallow let us have a sip of the wine he's mulling for them, too . . . oh, and Judd said there'd be a special surprise for us in the stables later," Tom chimed in.

Harriet shuddered at the catalogue of inappropriate delicacies the children had already consumed by half past seven in the morning. "Have you had any proper breakfast?" she inquired, reaching for the bell-pull beside her bed.

"Oh, Nurse Maddox made us eat porridge." Grace's nose wrinkled.

"But it did have raisins in it," her brother pointed out judiciously. "It was Christmas porridge, better than ordinary porridge."

"I suppose so," Grace conceded. "Oh, good morning, Agnes . . . will you hurry and help Harry to dress? We need to go down to Grandfather for our presents."

"Not until the Duke has had his breakfast, you don't," Harriet declared. "Otherwise there'll be no Christmas for anyone. Hurry back to the nursery, now, and let me dress in peace. I'll come up for you when it's time to go downstairs."

With only minor grumbles, they obeyed, and Agnes set a tray of hot chocolate and bread and butter on the bed. "Merry Christmas, m'lady."

Harriet returned the greeting, pouring a stream of fragrant chocolate into the shallow cup, while she previewed the day ahead. Agnes was stoking the fire, coaxing the embers into a roaring flame. "Will it be the emerald muslin for church, m'lady?"

"Yes, I think so, but I'll wear a woolen chemise and stockings. Otherwise I'll be an icicle before I even get to church, let alone sitting for an hour in a frigid pew." Harriet set aside her tray and got up from the bed. "The ermine pelisse as well, please, Agnes, with the matching muff. But first, would you pass me a dressing robe? I must go down and wish his grace a Merry Christmas before I do anything else."

Agnes held out the thick velvet robe and handed Harriet her fur-lined embroidered slippers. She brushed her mistress's hair and fastened it simply with a ribbon at the nape of her neck. Harriet glanced at her reflection and nodded. The Duke would not be looking for a fashion plate at his early-morning breakfast table.

She hurried downstairs and into the small parlor, where her grandfather chose to take breakfast away from his guests. She was surprised to see that Julius was at table with the Duke. "Merry Christmas, sir." She kissed her grandfather's cheek. "And to you, too, my lord." She nodded at the Earl. "I'm surprised you're up so early."

"Oh . . . how so?" He raised an eyebrow in that rather maddening way he had. "I didn't spend a night of dissolution, if that's what you're implying, ma'am. Any more than you did, if I may say so," he added with the hint of a question in his voice. And there was a look in the black eyes that unnerved her even more. It was a definite challenge. He couldn't possibly have known she had been following him the night before. Of course he couldn't.

"*I* certainly didn't, sir," she responded, unable to keep the slight emphasis from her voice, although she regretted it immediately. But his only response was a twitch of his raised eyebrow. "I was merely surprised that you should be down for breakfast," she went on hastily. "Except for the children, most people take breakfast in their rooms on Christmas morning."

"Total indolence," the Duke said, taking a draught of ale. "No time for this namby-pamby pandering. Where are the brats?"

"In the nursery, washing sugar off themselves, I hope," his granddaughter told him. "They've already consumed sugar plums, marzipan sheep, and mulled wine. I just hope they aren't violently sick in church."

"A little indulgence on this day of all days can do no harm, surely?" Julius inquired. "May I carve you some ham, Harriet?"

"That seems a small enough indulgence," she responded, unable to resist his sudden complicit smile. "Thank you."

Once again, he was enclosing them in their own little world. How did he do that? How could he annoy her one minute and the next make her feel that he was the most attractive man she had ever met? *Did he charm Nick in the same way? Charm him and then betray him?*

She sat down and buttered a piece of bread as Julius laid a wafer-thin slice of ham on her plate. She turned her attention away from that smile and those knowing black eyes. "Should you give the children their present before church, Grandfather? Judd has already warned them to expect a surprise in the stables."

"Then there'll be no holding them back," the Duke said. "Best before church, otherwise they'll never sit still through the sermon. Just hope old Greerson doesn't take it into his head to deliver one of his interminable sermons."

"I doubt he will." Harriet refilled her coffee cup. "He knows his congregation will be restless. Besides," she added with a chuckle, "he'll be as anxious to get up to the hall for his preprandial sherry as anyone else."

"That, my dear child, is the only comfort I have," the Duke declared, pushing back his chair. "If you'll both excuse me, I shall go and dress. You may bring the brats to the library in an hour, Harriet. We'll go to the stables then."

Julius rose politely as his host left the parlor, then resumed his seat. "So what awaits the twins in the stables?"

Harriet smiled. "Something that will send them into raptures and get them into all sorts of mischief. And it was Grandfather's idea, too." She shook her head with the same smile.

"And won't you enlighten me?" He was entranced by that smile, he realized. It transformed her usually grave expression, brought a glow to her creamy cheeks and a light to the green eyes that was sometimes as elusive as a will-o'-the-wisp. And he had the feeling that if he wasn't very careful she could lead him, like a will-o'-the-wisp, into the marshiest imbroglio.

"No, I won't spoil the surprise," she said on a sudden impulse. "Come with us to the stables, and you shall see for yourself . . . and be warned, you'll be experiencing the twins at their most unmanageable. Excitement has a dire effect on them."

"And you think I can handle such an experience?" he inquired, his lips twitching.

"Oh, eminently," she said with an airy wave as she rose from the table. "You do have the experience of your sister's children to fall back upon, after all. Even if you do have difficulty remembering how many of them there are." She went to the door, saying over her shoulder, "I have every faith in your resilience, my lord."

He had half risen from his chair as she made for the door and murmured with a bow, "You do me too much honor, my lady. I shall endeavor to earn it."

"Oh, I'm sure you'll do that with the greatest aplomb, sir." She gave another airy wave and left the parlor.

Julius sat down again and resumed his breakfast. There was no point denying the truth. He was not as in control of himself and his surroundings as he was accustomed to being. And for some strange reason, he didn't seem to mind. Perhaps the Christmas spirit had infected him.

Harriet reached her own chamber, wondering why she had issued that invitation. Julius Forsythe was not a member of the family, however familiarly he was treated by the Duke, and there was no more intimate family occasion than giving the children their Christmas presents. She sat down at the dresser while Agnes did her hair, looking into the mirror but not seeing herself. Nick's image came back at her instead. This was the first Christmas without him, and the hole he had left was impossible either to fill or to ignore for any one of them, and yet she had co-opted Julius to play Nick's role in the children's Christmas without a moment's hesitation. For Gracie and Tom . . . for the Duke . . . or for herself? She would have liked to believe it was an act of pure selflessness, but she had far too much integrity to ignore what she knew full well. It was as much for herself as for them. And it wasn't because Julius Forsythe took the place of Nick—of her brother—oh, no. There was no possible way Julius could in any way take Nick's place. He had his own. And it seemed to be setting down roots.

She dressed quickly, threw a cloak around her shoulders, and went up to the nursery, where, as she expected, the children, already dressed for the outdoors, were hopping from foot to foot, driving the nursery maids and Nurse Maddox to distraction. "Come, Grandfather is waiting for you." She took their hands firmly and led them down the nursery stairs to the main landing. "Now, try to be a little decorous, both of you."

"What's that . . . what's dec'rous?" Gracie demanded.

"Something that you are not," Harriet said, suppressing a smile.

"But something that you soon will be, Lady Grace," came the Earl's laughing voice from behind them.

Harriet turned around. He was looking very splendid in a black brocade coat with gold buttons, a gold striped waistcoat, and black britches. He carried a cloak loosely over his arm. "You are an optimist, Julius," she said lightly. "Make your curtsy, Gracie. It's customary when a lady receives a compliment."

Grace, looking a little shocked, bobbed a curtsy.

Tom offered a jerky bow, although his expression said that he was aware he had not received a compliment, however confusing.

"Lord Marbury is coming to the stables with us," Harriet told them as she encouraged them downstairs. "Remember to greet Grandfather properly, and don't say anything about presents . . . not until he mentions them first."

"That's what Nick always said . . . we remember," Tom declared, squaring his shoulders. Julius came up behind him and laid a hand on the thin shoulders and squeezed quickly, before letting his hand drop.

Harriet noticed but said nothing. It unsettled her when he acted like Nick around the children, as naturally as if he had lived in her brother's skin. And yet she was grateful for it.

The Duke was standing in front of the fireplace in the library when his grandchildren entered. The twins curtsied and bowed and murmured their greetings, their eyes darting sideways to their sister to see if they were doing it correctly. Their grandfather suddenly laughed. "Oh, you can't fool me, you rapscallions . . . butter wouldn't melt. Now, come here and give me a kiss and wish me a proper Merry Christmas." He held out his arms, and the children ran into them.

The Duke's eyes were a little wet as he hugged them to him.

"What did you get us for Christmas, Grandfather?" the twins demanded in unison, forgetting Harriet's injunction. They pranced around him.

"It's something in the stables, isn't it?" Tom said.

"Maybe it is, and maybe it isn't," the Duke said. "But first, you may give me your gifts."

The children proffered their own wrapped parcels, and their grandfather managed to look suitably delighted at a very ill-sewn sampler from Gracie and a wooden carving that with imagination could have been a ship from Tom. He set both with some ceremony on the mantelpiece and took a small package out of his coat pocket, turning to Harriet. "This was your grandmother's, my dear. I had the setting changed to suit more modern tastes."

Harriet took the tissue-wrapped package and opened it. It revealed a silver locket set with emeralds. She opened the locket, and her eyes filled as she looked upon the miniature of her brother, perfect in every detail. She had no words, but the Duke had no need of them and held her tight for a moment.

She gave him her own present, a beautifully illustrated copy of Milton's *Paradise Lost,* which she and

Nick had talked about buying for him together . . . before Nick had gone. It hadn't been easy buying it alone, but she had made herself do it, knowing it was something he would have wanted.

Julius stood to one side, making himself as inconspicuous as he could. He shouldn't be there, intruding on this family's most intimate memories, and yet he wanted to be there, to be part of Nick's family, perhaps in some way to help lessen the void of Nick's absence. He knew he could never really do that, but maybe there were little things he could do, although never enough to make up for what had happened that day in Bruges.

There was no way to make himself scarce without drawing attention to himself, so he kept still and silent until the moment of intensity had passed. Fortunately, the children knew how to hurry it on its way.

"May we go to the stables now, sir . . . Harry . . . *please,* may we?"

"Yes, I think you've waited long enough," the Duke said. "Come." He took a child by each hand, and they left the library through the French doors onto the terrace, making their way around the house to the stables.

Julius fell naturally into step with Harriet as they

followed the Duke and the dancing children. "I have a little gift for you myself," he said. "But I hesitate to present it at such a family occasion."

She turned to look up at him in surprise. "Oh, but you shouldn't . . . I don't have anything—"

"I don't expect you to," he interrupted swiftly. "I happened to see these in Oxford yesterday, and they seemed perfect for you." He took a package from his coat pocket. "They seem to be exactly the color of your eyes."

Harriet opened the paper carefully to reveal a pair of emerald-green doeskin riding gloves, edged with gold braid. She held them against her cheek, feeling their soft silkiness. "They're quite beautiful, Julius. How can I thank you?"

"Easily enough," he said, and without conscious thought bent to kiss the corner of her mouth. His tongue darted in a moist, intimate caress across her lips before he straightened, his dark eyes, although filled with light, regarding her with a startled question.

She swallowed. Her mouth felt deliciously warm, alive somehow. "Why did you do that?" It was all she could think of to say, and her gaze was as startled as his.

It was a question he was asking himself, but he heard himself answer, "Because I wanted to . . . I seem to have been wanting to kiss you since I first saw you." A rueful smile tugged at the corners of his mouth. "Do you mind?"

Harriet swallowed again, absently touching her lips with a gloved fingertip. "I don't know," she said truthfully. "It took me by surprise."

"If it's any consolation, it took *me* by surprise, too," he responded with the same rueful smile.

She glanced quickly at the stable yard and was relieved to see that her grandfather had his back to them and the children were hopping from foot to foot in anticipation, far too excited to notice anything untoward with their sister.

"Where is it?" Tom demanded. "I don't see anything."

"Just wait a minute," Harriet said, moving swiftly away from Julius. "Just listen."

They stopped hopping and stood stock-still, and then they heard the light tinkle of bells. Judd appeared around the corner of the stable block, leading a black pony with bells in its harness drawing a pony cart. The cart was painted crimson, and the pony's harness was tooled emerald-green leather.

"Is it ours?" Grace asked, her mouth half-open.

"Just for us . . . our very own carriage?" Tom sounded awed.

"Yes," her grandfather assured them, smiling. "Your very own carriage, and you shall both learn to drive it. Judd will teach you. I expect you both to turn into fine whips by the spring."

"Oh, we will . . . we will." The pair of them, chanting in unison, ran to the pony and cart and within minutes were arguing about names for the pony.

"A success, I think," the Duke stated. "And if they have yours and your brother's natural ability with the reins, they should be driving themselves around the estate in a few months."

"Not without a groom," Harriet said swiftly.

"No," the Duke agreed. "Most definitely not without a groom, and I think it would be wise if some kind of schedule were drawn up as to who should have the reins and when. Otherwise there'll be nothing but arguments."

"I will see to it, sir," Harriet said, catching a quick frowning glance from the Earl, which puzzled her. It seemed almost disapproving. She turned her attention back to the children, who were leading the pony around the yard under Judd's supervision. "I think I'll save my presents until after church," she said. "They have enough to feast on for the moment."

"I'll go back to the house. We should leave for church in half an hour, Harriet. Make sure they're clean and tidy." He strode off, his thick mane of white hair catching the winter sunlight.

"Anyone would think you were their governess," Julius said abruptly, his voice rather clipped. "Is there no one else responsible for them?"

"Yes, of course there is," Harriet said, somewhat defensively. "Nursemaids, governess, tutor. My grandfather just relies on me to organize them, that's all."

He didn't say anything, but his thick black eyebrows were still drawn together in a frown. He left her and walked over to the children, who were scrambling into the pony cart, already squabbling over who was to take the reins. He stopped at the cart, one hand resting along the side, and said something to the twins that Harriet couldn't hear. They stopped squabbling, however, and Tom passed the reins to his sister, who, after practicing holding them for a few minutes, passed them back to her brother. Julius nodded and left them, returning to where Harriet still stood watching.

"It seems you can perform miracles, my lord," Harriet said lightly. "They actually listened to you."

"I find most people do," he responded with what she thought was infuriating complacence. And then he grinned at her. "That annoyed you, didn't it?"

She couldn't help laughing. "Yes, it did. How smug you sounded."

"Well, it seems to be a natural response when you call me *my lord* in that supercilious voice," he replied. "I become smug." He reached out a hand and lightly caressed her cheek with a fingertip. It seemed an almost careless gesture, and yet her cheek came alive beneath the stroking touch, and she felt her stomach lurch with a strange surge of excitement. Her eyes were locked with his for an interminable moment. Somehow that earlier brushing kiss had altered the balance between them. Even the air around them felt different, charged in some way, so that the intimate fingertip caress felt natural, inevitable.

"Harry, Harry, look, we're driving!" The excited shriek from the twins shattered the moment, and she turned with mingled relief and disappointment away from Julius, giving her attention to the children, who were slowly driving the pony cart around the yard.

Julius stood to one side, his arms folded, watching her. She was hatless, and her gleaming fair hair was simply dressed in a braided knot at the nape of her neck, delicate side ringlets framing her face. It was a style that in profile showed her very firm pointed chin and the smooth, straight nose to perfection. Her cloak hung open from her slim shoulders, and sideways he could see the swell of her breast above the high waist-line of her emerald velvet gown.

His body stirred. Every rational instinct told him that she was out of bounds. He was on a mission, one that at his very core he believed to be the most important of his life. He owed it to Nick to succeed, and now he was contemplating jeopardizing that mission for Nick's sister. But he couldn't seem to help himself. The iron control he had developed over his emotions, his needs outside his work, had stood him in good stead over the years, and now he felt it slipping. It frightened him, and yet he saw an oddly liberating vista opening before him.

Afterwards, after he had done what he had to do, maybe he could revisit that vista. But until then, he needed to reestablish that control.

Chapter Nine

Julius had joined the church party gathered in the hall when Harriet, wearing an ermine pelisse, her hands buried in an ermine muff, came down the stairs with the children, once more tidy and scrubbed. He crossed to the staircase and gave her his hand down the last step. It was such a natural gesture she thought nothing of it, taking her hand from her muff and placing it in his. Only then did she remember that she had told herself very firmly that she needed to step back from Julius Forsythe, keep a distance between them that would prevent any further sudden intimacies. And yet in the last few minutes, that resolution seemed to have dissolved like sugar in hot water. In the same way, she could find no sufficient reason for them not to walk together to church, at the rear of the procession, the children running a little ahead of them.

"When do you plan to return to London?" Harriet asked. "You must have friends . . . people to see, things to do." Maybe, she told herself, she could maintain a distance with casual conversation, even while she directed the conversation into avenues that might prove enlightening.

"Oh, I'm in no hurry," he responded with a careless shrug. "The Duke has been kind enough to extend an open invitation, and in truth, the country life suits me. I enjoy the hunt, and I'm quite a fair shot, and I don't mind my own company."

For some reason, this didn't surprise Harriet. He seemed so self-contained. "Do you know people in Oxford? When you went there yesterday afternoon, did you visit friends?"

"No," he responded, glancing down at her. "As I believe I told you, I went into the town just to revisit old memories. And they didn't come up to expectations, as I believe I also told you."

"Oh, did you?" she said vaguely. "I forgot."

Like hell you did. He made no further comment, however, and waited with some interest to see what she would come up with next.

Harriet cursed her clumsiness. She really wasn't very good at this. She'd asked the question hoping it would lead to something, but that was idiotic. She was dealing with a professional. He wasn't going to give something away inadvertently. "I just wondered if there was anyone left over from your student days, someone who had stayed on after his degree, teaching perhaps." She offered an indifferent shrug as if the issue were of no real interest.

"Not that I know of," Julius said.

"Nick still had many friends even after he went down," she persevered. "But then, of course, he grew up only ten miles from the city, so perhaps it's not that surprising."

"No," he agreed. "Not in the least surprising. Besides, your brother seemed to make friends very easily."

"And you don't." It was more of a statement than a question.

"No," he agreed again. The questions were coming a little close to home. A man in his line of work couldn't afford friendships.

"And yet . . . and yet you and Nick became friends, good friends." She glanced at him, watching his expression, which seemed suddenly to have closed.

"As you say" was his only response.

Harriet's attention was suddenly diverted to Tom, who was walking just a little in front of her. She had been noticing rather absently that his hand was constantly going to the back pocket of his nankeen britches. She looked closely for a moment and then said, "Oh, I don't believe it. Today of all days. Wretched boy."

"What?" Julius asked, his step slowing.

"Tom's got something in his back pocket, and it's alive," she said with a sigh. "Look, you can see it moving."

Julius followed her gaze and saw what she meant. Tom's back pocket was squirming as if with a life of its own.

"I'd better deal with it before we get any closer to the church," Harriet said, increasing her pace to catch up with the twins. "Whatever he's up to, it's bound to cause a massive scene, and Grandfather will be furious."

Julius put a restraining hand on her arm. "My dear girl, you have far too much responsibility for those children. You can't anticipate every little thing. Let Tom discover the consequences of his actions for himself for once."

"I can't," she said, setting her lips. "Not yet. The Duke's just waiting for a reason to pack him off to school, and he's not ready." Another sigh escaped her. "I do miss Nick. He always dealt with this kind of thing."

Julius looked at her strangely, a mixture of compassion and something that for a second she almost thought was remorse. Then he said, "Just leave it to me." He walked quickly up to Tom, taking his arm and drawing him firmly off the narrow path and into the bushes alongside. They were out of sight for a few minutes, and then Tom reappeared, looking rather subdued, to join his twin, followed by Julius, who rejoined Harriet.

"What was it?" she asked in a low voice.

"A mouse. It's gone now."

"Oh, dear." Harriet put a hand over her mouth to stop the laughter that threatened to convulse her. "Just think of what a mouse in church would have done to the aunts." It was too much, and she yielded to the gale of amusement that broke from her.

Julius looked at her in astonishment. "What on earth can you find to laugh about? A minute ago, you were at your wit's end."

She controlled the bubbles of laughter and said

rather more soberly, "I know, but you see, since Nick died, the twins had stopped playing their tricks. They hardly got into mischief at all. They've been so sad, although they've kept it to themselves most of the time. But that . . . well, that was the old Tom, the one who was always up to something, and it's such a relief to me. It means they're getting over the worst of their grief."

Julius was silent for a moment, and she couldn't know that he was struggling with the extraordinary urge to hold her tightly to him, to kiss those paper-thin eyelids, to whisper assurances that she didn't carry the burdens of her brother's death alone.

"We need to hurry," she said into the silence. "There are the bells." She moved ahead of him to catch up with the children, taking their hands.

"Sorry, Harry," Tom said, looking up at her.

"For what?" she asked with a smile. "The mouse?"

"Well, that, too, but for making life difficult for you. Lord Marbury said we both did and we have to stop."

"I think Great-aunt Augusta would probably swoon if she saw a mouse, don't you, Harry?" Grace asked.

"Quite likely," Harriet agreed drily, hurrying them

through the lych-gate and up the path to the church doors. "So it's fortunate she won't."

Julius followed them into the dim, incense-scented church just as the bells stopped ringing. The verger closed the doors firmly as Julius slid into the pew next to Tom. Harriet couldn't help a little mental sigh of relief as she saw him take his place. The children were imprisoned between them, just as they always had been between herself and Nick. For the next hour, she could relax her vigilance and let her mind wander through the service.

But her mind had only one path of choice, it seemed. The man singing carols in a powerful and re-markably melodious baritone at the end of the pew. What was he? A traitor, a betrayer, a deceiver, an as-sassin? Could such a man also show a deep well of strength and compassion? Could such a man actually be as attractive, as sensual, as utterly appealing as she found Julius Forsythe to be? Was she in the grip of some strange enchantment that drowned her doubts, somehow made nothing of the facts she knew about the man, rendered her powerless to resist his appeal?

Was he responsible for Nick's death?

How could he have been when he seemed so eas-ily to slip into Nick's skin, or at least his family role?

Even the Duke seemed to view him as some kind of a substitute for Nick. But then, if he was what the Ministry suspected, a double agent working with the French, his cover depended upon his gaining the trust and liking of Nick's family so that he could enjoy their hospitality and pursue his own traitorous course from the safe house they provided for him. In order to use them, he had to have their friendship.

And that thought filled her with white-hot rage once more. As it surged through her, she heard her own voice raised in song, every word a stab of fury aimed at the man at the end of the pew.

And then the carol came to an end, and she became aware of heads and puzzled glances turned in her direction and realized that she must have been singing so loudly she'd drawn attention to herself. She sat down abruptly and buried her head in her hymnal as the vicar climbed into the pulpit for his Christmas sermon.

If only she could find definitive proof, one way or another, of the Earl's guilt or innocence. Would he return to the clearing in the woods? What had the hieroglyphic on the tree meant? Or, rather, whom was it meant for? If she could discover that, she would find her answer.

"That's quite a voice to emerge from such a dainty frame," Julius observed as they finally made their way back out into the frosty air. "You were singing to bring down the rafters."

"You're not exactly a whisperer yourself," she retorted, feeling herself flush, annoyed that he had noticed her outburst, but then, so had everyone else in the church, she reminded herself.

"True enough, but no one would call my frame dainty," he pointed out with a humorous glint in his eye.

"No, I suppose they wouldn't," Harriet conceded. "Mind you, I don't consider myself to be particularly dainty."

"Well, believe me, dear girl, you are. Delectably so."

It took her a moment to recover from this openly flirtatious gambit. "Permit me to inform you, my lord, that that is a most indelicate remark."

"Oh, you're being supercilious again," he chided, still with that humorous glint in his eye. "Delectably dainty and annoyingly supercilious."

"You're the only person who thinks so," she responded.

"Really?" His eyebrows lifted in question. "Which facet, delectably dainty or annoyingly supercilious?"

"Oh, do stop playing silly games. I don't find them in the least amusing." She increased her pace as if she could leave him behind, but he kept pace easily, lengthening his stride.

"I only play silly games with supercilious women," he said. "Now, cry truce, Harriet. I was merely paying you a compliment."

"An indelicate one," she muttered, unwilling to give up just yet, her earlier surge of rage still simmering.

"Very well, if you say so." He drew her hand out of her muff and tucked it into his elbow. "Let us walk on in a decorous fashion, exchanging amiable and unobjectionable small talk, if that is your wish."

An inconvenient bubble of laughter came to her lips, and she fought it down. She didn't want to encourage him, but he *did* make her laugh, and then she got confused all over again.

"That's better," he said encouragingly. "You want to smile, and you're trying not to, but I should inform you that you have an entrancing smile. You should show it to the world more often, you know."

His tone was that of a kindly uncle dispensing advice, and it proved too much for Harriet's gravity. She laughed and felt a curious lightness in her chest, a sense of losing some burden, as if the rage had finally gone from her, which was ridiculous because nothing had happened to change that moment in church.

"*Much* better," he said, patting her hand as it rested in the crook of his arm. "Now, tell me what to expect for the rest of the day."

It was no good. She couldn't possibly keep up her anger or even a semblance of annoyance. She gave in with a good grace and explained the day's program to him. "What kind of a card player are you, by the way?" she asked as she finished her description.

"Adequate," he said. "Why?"

"Because there will be tables for whist and piquet set up after the feast. It's the one compensation the Duke has, apart from tomorrow's hunt, for entertaining all these relatives whom he generally despises. The great-aunts are rather good whist players."

"And you?" he asked.

"Adequate," she responded.

"Then perhaps we should engineer to play as partners. That way, we won't annoy anyone by trumping their ace or some other solecism."

"You wouldn't do such a thing?" she exclaimed,

then shook her head. "No, you can't fool me. I cannot believe there is anything you do that you fail to do superbly."

His eyes seemed to darken even more than usual. "Oh, you mistake, my dear. You give me too much credit. In some things, I have failed miserably."

"Such as?" She asked the question without giving herself time to think about it.

His eyes moved away from her to some point in the distance. His mouth had hardened, and she felt a faint shiver of apprehension. Whatever he was looking at, she had no wish to see it herself. Then he shrugged and said easily, "Oh, divided loyalties are the very devil, didn't you say that yourself, my dear?"

She had done. And now he was admitting he struggled with them. Was that as good as an admission of following two masters? But it wasn't, of course. Harriet had her own divided loyalties, and she certainly wasn't betraying anyone. "I suppose we all have them," she said as easily as he.

They had reached the house, and Harriet went upstairs to take off her outdoor clothes. The local dignitaries were gathering in the great hall for their traditional Christmas drink with the Duke and his family, but she knew she could safely leave their entertainment to her grandfather and, on this occasion, the great-aunts, who enjoyed welcoming their social inferiors with ample condescension.

The children had been whisked to the nursery to be dressed for their appearance in the dining room, and she had a few minutes to herself. She sat at her dresser and examined herself critically in the glass. She thought she looked surprisingly well. The tiny lines of strain that so often these days appeared around her mouth and at the corners of her eyes were nowhere to be seen. Indeed, her eyes seemed larger and more lustrous than usual. And her skin had a dewy pink glow to it, presumably from the walk in the frosty air. But perhaps there was another cause. Perhaps it had something to do with that lightness that persisted in her chest. With the sense of her skin being somehow alive. With the feeling of energy that coursed through her. At that moment, Harriet didn't think there was anything she could not do, any problem she could not solve. Any fence she could not jump. She was quite simply exhilarated.

And that was a feeling she realized she had not experienced since she had been given the news of Nick's death.

The feeling persisted throughout the rest of the

day, through the "Boar's Head Carol" that heralded the beginning of the feast, through the interminable meal, the constant flow of claret, the long
afternoon and evening of cards, piquet, and back-
gammon. She seemed to be aware of Julius at every
moment, whether he was at her side during dinner
or elsewhere making polite conversation with other
members of the party. He performed his social obli-
gations remarkably well for a self-confessed lover of
his own company. And she had been right about his
ability with cards. She watched with admiration as
somehow, when it came to drawing partners, he en-
gineered the cutting of cards so that they drew each
other.

"What did you do?" she whispered as they moved
around the table to take their places. "Some sleight of
hand, I know it."

He merely gave her an enigmatic smile and held
out the chair of the lady to his right. He played
without expression, calling his bid, laying down his
card, once or twice glancing at her when she called
a bid as if reading her expression for clues. He certainly seemed to read correctly, because they rose
the winners by a handsome sum at the end of the
evening. Harriet knew she was quite a good player,

but she had never been as good as when she was playing to Lord Marbury's lead.

The party began to break up close to midnight, and Julius accompanied Harriet into the hall to the table at the foot of the stairs, where the carrying candles were set out around a blazing candelabra. He lit one for her and gave it to her, his fingers for a second closing around her wrist. "Good night, my lady." A smile flickered across his eyes, touched the corners of his mouth. "My thanks for a profitable evening."

"Good night, my lord." She curtsied demurely. "It would not have been so profitable if I had not been playing with an expert."

"You flatter me, my dear. You follow a lead to perfection." He lifted her free hand to his lips. "Sleep well."

"I shall. For those who wish to hunt, breakfast will be served at seven in the dining room. Should you wish for anything earlier, you have only to inform Thomas."

"Could you pretend, for just a few moments, that you are not in charge of this entire production?" he asked, his voice still low. "Not for a minute do you let it go."

"I don't know how to," she responded, now with

a touch of acerbity. "It's been my responsibility since I put up my hair. It's second nature, and believe it or not, sir, I enjoy it." She dropped another curtsy, an ironic one this time, and twitched her hand free of his fingers. "I bid you good night, Lord Marbury."

"Lady Harriet." He bowed to her departing back as she swept up the stairs. Why did it bother him so, this huge responsibility that she took with such seeming ease on those slender shoulders? At her age, she should be dancing the night away at some ball somewhere, flirting with possible suitors. She would have flocks of eligible young men at her feet if she chose to lift a finger. With her beauty, her fortune, her lineage, she was every young man's dream. And every potential mother-in-law's dreams for her son.

Instead, she chose to make something of a recluse of herself, running a huge household, tending to her grandfather's whims, and steering a pair of unruly brats out of trouble whenever possible. But grief did things to people. Although she no longer wore mourning for her brother, Julius knew she was still raw with her sorrow. He could see it in her eyes, feel it in her body when he stood close to her.

And there was nothing he could do to assuage it. He, of all people, was helpless in this.

Chapter Ten

Harriet had told Agnes she would need no help un-
dressing that night. She didn't want to interrupt the
girl's Christmas festivities in the servants' hall, but
she also had her own plans. She went to the window,
drawing back the heavy curtain to look out at the
darkened garden. It was another frosty moonlit night,
the woods looming black shadows along the edge of
the lawn.

The idea to explore on her own had formed itself
at some point in the evening. Why should she not
go to the clearing and see if the hieroglyphic was still
there or if something had been added to it? She would
transcribe the markings and have something to offer
the Ministry. They might well have meaning for the

experts even if they meant nothing to her. It would be something concrete to show them at the very least.

She changed out of her evening gown and dressed in her riding habit. It was warmer and sturdier than indoor garments, and her boots would keep her feet dry in the frosty grass, where silk slippers would not. She slung a heavy hooded cloak around her shoulders, tucked a piece of parchment and a pencil into the deep pocket of the cloak, and softly let herself out of her chamber. The sound of music and laughter still rose from the servants' hall, but the house lights had been extinguished except for a wall sconce at the head of the main staircase that offered some illumination.

The front doors had been locked and barred for the night, so Harriet let herself out by a side door. Leaving the door unlocked, she moved quickly, hugging the shadows of the bushes that lined the narrow gravel path. She couldn't imagine that anyone would be looking down on the path from the house, but there was something about slipping out in the dark on a clandestine mission that made her extra cautious. She had every right to be anywhere she chose, in or out of the house, at whatever time of day or night, but that knowledge didn't lessen the sense of apprehension, the knowledge that one person, at least, would object to what she was doing. Julius had never behaved in her company in a manner that could be called at all threatening, but there was something about him, a look she had occasionally seen in his eye, that made her certain she did not want to fall foul of him.

She kept to the shadow of the trees alongside the lawn until she reached the alley that led into the woods. It was darker in there, and she hesitated. Perhaps she should have brought flint and tinder to light a taper. If it was pitch dark, how would she see the marking on the tree clearly enough to transcribe it? But as she stared into the darkness and her eyes became accustomed, she realized that there was a grayish tinge to the blackness and the leafless trees were allowing some moonlight onto the alley. She set off again with more confidence, her footsteps almost silent on the mossy ground.

She thought she heard a twig snap and stopped, her heart pounding. But then there was silence, followed by a rustle in the undergrowth alongside the path. Of course, the woods were alive at night. A hunting owl hooted, and then came the faint scream of some small animal. She shivered a little. Even though she had been born and bred in the country, there was something menacing about the woods at night.

She came to the first clearing and crossed it quickly. Then, instead of taking the smaller pathway to the next clearing, she slipped into the trees to approach it from an angle. Why, she wasn't sure, an innate caution. Something was going on in these woods that concerned Julius Forsythe. He may or may not be a double agent, but she knew he was a spy. An assassin, too. It went with the territory.

She moved stealthily from tree trunk to tree trunk as she got closer to the second clearing. The ground was littered with twigs and dead leaves, and her booted feet were not quite as silent as they had been on the mossy path. Every snapped twig, every crunch of a dried leaf sounded to her like a clash of cymbals. Anyone in the clearing would know that someone was coming, and her heart seemed to lodge itself in her throat. The pulse drumming in her ears seemed to drown out all else, and she stopped abruptly behind the broad trunk of an ancient oak to take a deep calming breath and listen intently.

As the drumming pulse in her ears slowed, she could hear the soft sounds of the bubbling spring, and then the customary woodland sounds came alive around her. The small clearing opened just ahead of her, lit by a shaft of moonlight that cast an eerie silver glow over the mossy carpet. And then she saw it. A dark shadow moved across the shaft of light. A slight figure in black. Too slight to be Julius.

Harriet bit her lip hard as she fought the urge to slip backwards through the trees to the safety of the house. She was there to get information, at the very least to make a copy of the marking on the tree. She couldn't give up at this stage. The figure was out of sight when she crept forward on tiptoe to the next tree trunk, praying she wouldn't tread on anything that would make a noise. The trunk was not as broad as the oak behind her, but she hoped it gave her sufficient coverage while enabling her to see further into the clearing.

The slight black-clad figure was standing motionless at the edge of the moonlight, looking at the tree with the marking. Then, swiftly, he obliterated the chalk mark with his gloved hand and turned back to face the clearing, leaning backwards against the tree as if he were waiting for something . . . or someone.

Harriet remained still, barely breathing, watching the clearing. She had no hope of reconstructing the marking now, but something was about to happen. Whatever the man was waiting for, she would wait for it, too. And then Julius walked into the moonlight. There was nothing stealthy in the way he strode confidently into the clearing. The figure against the tree came forward, and they both stood in the moonlight.

"*Bonsoir, Marcel.*" Julius greeted the man with a brief handshake.

"*Bonsoir, Javier, mon ami. C'est bien?*"

"*Oui, c'est bien.*" Julius took something from the inside pocket of his coat and gave it to his companion, who slipped it inside his cloak. There was another brief handshake, and the Frenchman vanished from the moonlight into the trees.

Julius stood where he was, absolutely motionless, as if he were listening for something . . . waiting for something to happen. Harriet stopped breathing altogether, shrinking into the tree that shielded her. Julius looked slowly around him, still without moving. Then he stepped quickly to the tree that he had marked and examined it closely. He gave it a final rub with his own gloved hand and retraced his steps across the clearing and disappeared into the trees.

Harriet remained where she was. If she waited twenty minutes, Julius would be comfortably back in the house and in his chamber by the time she reached the house herself.

She had her evidence now. Julius, Julius who was also called Javier, had met with a Frenchman, a French spy. He had given him information, or whatever was contained in the packet now securely in the enemy agent's possession. And all she felt was a disappointment so deep tears pricked behind her eyes. It was suddenly very cold in the woods, and she realized she had been so keyed up with excitement and apprehension she hadn't noticed the drop in temperature. She began to shiver almost uncontrollably and, without further thought, turned and plunged back into the woods, heedless of the noise her feet made as she blundered back to the larger clearing.

She emerged into the garden a few minutes later. The moon was obscured by clouds now, and she didn't trouble to keep to the shadows of the hedge alongside the path. Julius had to be back in the house by now. She hurried for the side door and reached for the latch.

The door was locked.

She stood for a moment, puzzled. She had left it unlocked. Could one of the servants have been checking the doors before going to bed? But no, not on Christmas night. They were too busy enjoying their own festivities to worry about something as mundane as rechecking what would already have been done. She tried the latch again, and the door opened with such suddenness she reared back.

"Well, well, and what little adventuress is this? What took you out on this frosty midnight, my dear?" Julius drawled, holding the door open but not wide enough for her to sweep past him. He was still dressed in coat and boots, holding his gloves in one hand. His black eyes were as cold as the frigid night air, and the smile on his finely drawn mouth was a travesty of his usual warm, humorous quirk. "Or should I say whom?" he added, moving very slightly, just enough to give her entrance. "An assignation, perhaps?"

Harriet half pushed, half sidled past him into the corridor, acutely aware of every line of his body. "I fail to see what business my actions are of yours, Lord Marbury." She was relieved to hear that her voice was quite steady, although inside she felt as wobbly as a bowl of blancmange. But her anger and disappointment enabled her to push through her fear and greet him with the hauteur that she could always rely upon to keep distance between them.

His eyes narrowed. The way he was standing blocked her way down the corridor to the freedom of the wide expanse of the great hall. She was pent up in the corridor, with the side door at her back and the Earl's powerful frame in front of her. She had never found him intimidating before, but now she knew a stab of genuine fear. It was ridiculous, of course. What could he do to her, here in her own home? But he radiated menace.

"So?" he queried, not moving. "Was it an assignation, my lady? A lover, perhaps? One who would be persona non grata under your grandfather's roof?"

There was mockery in his voice, and she flushed with anger, her fear vanishing. "Maybe I should ask the same question of you, sir?" she retorted, her eyes flashing green fire. "Or should I say Javier?"

He shook his head. "I doubt that would be wise." Almost indolently, he reached out and hooked a finger in the clasp of her cloak at her throat and drew her towards him until she was standing so close she could feel the heat of his body, the contained power in his body. With his free hand, he cupped her chin and lifted her face. "You really should not meddle in things beyond your ken, my dear."

His black gaze was furious, his fingers on her chin pressing hard, and Harriet felt she was in the presence of a stranger, and then something happened. She could feel the air shift between them in an almost palpable current, and behind the anger in his eyes shone something else, a deep, dark glow of a passion that superseded anger.

"Oh, God, woman, what are you doing to me?" he murmured, sounding almost helpless, but there was nothing helpless about his mouth on hers.

Her lips burned under the pressure of a kiss that was not quite a kiss, more of a statement of some kind. Confusion swamped her. She didn't know whether she wanted to push him away or pull him closer, and through the muddle of sensation, she felt his mouth on hers became softer and yet more insistent. She could smell the winter-fresh scent of his skin, the faint lavender fragrance of the linen press rising from his shirt, and the warmth of his body seemed to envelop her. And there was no longer confusion, just this engulfing desire that thrummed deep within her body.

Julius moved his hand from her chin, caressing the line of her jaw, the curve of her cheekbones. His tongue stroked her lips, pressed for entrance. Her lips parted for him, and he moved within the warm softness of her mouth, stroking the inside of her cheek, his tongue fencing delicately with hers. Harriet found it an entrancing sensation, so startlingly intimate and yet somehow so natural. The sweetness of cognac lingered on his tongue.

Where the bee sucks, there suck I . . .

The quote from *The Tempest* drifted into her head, and she wanted to laugh with delight even as she leaned into his embrace. His arms were around her, holding her beneath her cloak, his hands moving down her back, over the curve of her hips, pressing her against his own hard body. And then he drew back, still holding her hips as he looked at her.

"Oh, damn," he murmured. "That was never meant to happen, but you do weave sweet magic."

"You were angry," she reminded him softly, touching her lips, trying to read his expression.

"Yes, I was." He sighed but didn't release his hold on her hips. "You don't know what you're meddling in, Harriet."

"Then tell me." It was a challenge.

He shook his head. "It's not mine to tell, Harriet."

"Did you kill Nick?" The question came without volition. But suddenly, it seemed the only important one.

The silence seemed to stretch interminably, as taut as a thread pulled to breaking point. Then his hands fell from her body, and he turned away, walking quickly to the darkened hall. Harriet stood still and watched until the shadows swallowed him. Why hadn't he answered her? Even a *yes* would have been a relief, anything but this dreadful uncertainty, the doubt, the hope. How could she feel this way for someone who had murdered her brother? She couldn't. It wasn't possible. But he hadn't denied it.

She went upstairs slowly. The fire was dying, and she replenished it, watching the fresh logs catch and blaze. Slowly, she undressed and was dropping her nightgown over her head when her chamber door flew open.

Chapter Eleven

"No," Julius stated, coming into the chamber, kicking the door shut behind him. "No, I did not kill Nick." He came over to her where she stood. The folds of the nightgown rippled around her as it fell to cover her body. He wore only his britches and shirt, his feet bare, his hair slightly rumpled as if he'd been running his hands through it.

"I didn't think you could have," she said softly. "I couldn't feel this way if you had." The chamber seemed to lose the hard contours of reality, to waver at the edges. It was as if she were entering some dreamland, a land that had been waiting just beyond the horizon, one where ordinary rules did not apply, where what one did in the real world became irrelevant.

There was only this, this breathless moment when everything stood still, and the deep, powerful wanting grew and grew until it filled every inch of her.

He lifted her against him, holding her up for a moment, and then took a step to the bed and dropped her onto the coverlet. He looked down at her as she lay, gazing up at him, her green eyes candid with desire. "I don't know what magic you weave, Harriet, but you have me in thrall," he murmured. "Never have I felt this way before."

The words caressed her, filled her with a sense of her own power, a newfound power. Her body began to sing beneath his languorous gaze as he ran his eyes over her, keeping his hands at his sides. His dark eyes had that deep velvety texture again. She could see herself reflected in the rich black pools, and she seemed to lose the shape of her self in their depths. She moved against the coverlet, her legs parting slightly of their own volition, a strange liquid weakness filling her loins and belly.

He put one knee on the bed beside her and leaned over, his mouth locking onto hers. Her lips parted instantly, and this time she was the aggressor, her tongue darting between his lips, touching, playing with his, her mouth filled with sweetness. His hand was on her breast, outlined beneath the thin lace-edged muslin of her nightgown, and she felt her nipple harden, pressing against the material up into his palm. He smiled against her mouth and raised his head, moving his free hand to her other breast, watching her face as he teased the nipple through her gown, feeling it harden with its twin. He bent his head again and pressed his lips against the fast-beating pulse in her throat as his hands continued their slow caress of her breasts.

A soft moan escaped her, and she stretched her body on the bed, her back arching slightly as if she could press her breasts even further into his hands. She reached up, her hands twisting in his thick dark hair, pulling his head up higher so that she could find his mouth with hers again, filled with an invincible hunger that she couldn't name.

"Slowly," he whispered, moving his mouth to her cheek, his tongue delicately stroking the curve of her cheek, before touching her eyelids, each one in turn, in a dainty butterfly kiss that brought every nerve ending in her skin to life. He lifted his head, looking into her eyes, a searching question in his dark gaze.

She met his look, reading the question. "I want this," she said simply. "I know I want this." She had never felt like this before, wasn't even sure what it was she was feeling, but Harriet knew it was right, knew that if he left her now, the emptiness of disappointment would be almost unendurable. At this moment, nothing else mattered.

He nodded, his gaze clearing, his eyes suddenly bright and focused. He unfastened his shirt, sliding it off his shoulders, letting it fall to the floor. He unbuttoned his britches and pushed them off his hips, showing himself to her, his penis jutting from the nest of black curls at the apex of his thighs.

Harriet looked at it, imagined that hard length entering her body. A warm flush crept over her skin, and the liquid fullness in her loins intensified. *What will it feel like?* She understood the basic mechanics of the business—for that, she had country life to thank—but she had no idea beyond that. She had never had anyone to ask.

Julius bent over her, taking the hem of her nightgown with one hand, sliding it up the length of her legs, his other hand stroking her bare skin as it was revealed inch by inch. When the gown reached the top of her thighs, she inhaled sharply, and he paused, his intent gaze on her face once more. Her tongue touched her lips, and she let her muscles relax, her legs sinking into the bed as the tension flowed from her.

As he felt her relax, he raised the nightgown another inch, and another. She felt the air on her belly, felt his eyes on her nakedness, his hand stroking upwards across her belly as he raised the gown further. There was a moment when he slid a hand intimately beneath her, cupping her bottom as he lifted her hips to free the matcrial, then let her relax back onto the mattress. Within seconds, the air was cool and yet warm on her bared breasts, her nipples hard and erect beneath his stroking hands. He lowered his head, and his tongue took the place of his hands in a moist, teasing caress over the swell of her breasts. His teeth lightly grazed her nipples, and she was aware of a deep tug in her belly, a wash of warmth in her loins. A little whimper of pleasure broke from her.

He moved onto the bed, kneeling astride her, lifting her nightgown up over her head, sliding a hand beneath her head to lift it free. Then he sat back on his heels and gazed at her as she lay spread out in front of him. A smile touched his lips. "Do you know how very beautiful you are, Harriet? You are so lovely."

Her pleasure deepened at the wonder in the rich, melodious voice, and she felt herself to be every bit as lovely as he said. She wanted to touch him as he had touched her and tentatively reached a hand to his penis, touching the tip with her fingertip, looking at him as she did so.

"Please," he murmured with the same smile. "Learn the feel of me. It will only increase the pleasure for both of us."

Emboldened by his words and by her own sudden need, she enclosed him in her fist, feeling the corded veins pulse against her palm. It was so strong, so muscular, so full of a life of its own. Instinctively, she moved her hand between his thighs, cupping the hard sacs at the base of his penis, and this time, it was Julius who groaned, his head falling back as her hands continued to explore the feel of him. Once again, she gloried in this sense of power, this knowledge that she could give him such pleasure just with her touch. Her hips shifted on the coverlet in involuntary invitation.

Slowly, Julius put his hand between her thighs, a finger sliding deep into the cleft of her sex. She gasped, shocked by the invasion and yet filled with a deep sensual delight. He continued to move his finger, watching her face, feeling her moistness. "This is the first time for you?" The sound of his voice was startling in the intense silence of their play. It was part question, part statement, and Harriet just nodded.

"Trust me, sweetheart," he said softly, bending

to kiss her. As his lips met hers, his stroking finger slipped suddenly inside her. She gasped once against his mouth at the suddenness of the intrusion, at the initial stab of pain. His finger moved swiftly, easing higher into her body, and the cry broke from her as the pain intensified, something seemed to stretch and break within her, and then it was over. He withdrew his finger gently and slipped his hands beneath her bottom, lifting her onto the shelf of his palms. "It will be easier for you this way."

His intent gaze was on her face, reading her expression as he pushed inside the tight sheath of her body. She licked her dry lips, her eyes never leaving his, hanging on to his gaze as if to a lifeline. He was filling her up, and yet there was no pain now and only momentary discomfort before her body opened around him. She didn't move, her mind and body focused on these new sensations, on the quivering deep in her belly, the tautness in her thighs. He moved with a slow, steady rhythm, pressing deeper, then withdrawing a little, and each time, she felt herself open further, until she instinctively moved her own hips, establishing her own rhythm in time with his. He smiled down at her and bent his head to kiss her, a deep and lingering kiss, as he continued to move within her.

Harriet put her hands on his back, then down to his buttocks, feeling the hard muscles against her palm as he drove the rhythm. Abruptly, his movements increased, and the quivering in her belly grew stronger. She tightened her thighs, lifted her hips a fraction higher. For a moment, she was as taut as a bow string. Julius withdrew to the very edge of her body, his eyes never leaving her face. Then he drove into her, and she felt as if she were shattering into a million pieces. He withdrew from her with a short, sharp cry and buried his face in her shoulder.

She felt the warmth of his seed on her belly and thighs, the pulsing moisture of her own core, as she lay spread-eagled, drained, filled with the deepest and sweetest weakness. Her hands stroked down his back, her fingers pushing into his hair as his head lay heavy on her shoulder, until he shifted to the bed beside her, one leg still across her, pinning her hips to the bed.

After a moment, he moved his leg and hitched himself onto an elbow. He looked down at her, a slight smile playing over his lips as he stroked the fair hair from her face. "How are you?"

"I think I'm all here," she murmured, her own smile still rather weak. "For a moment, I seemed to be in a million pieces."

"You are an amazing woman." He kissed her, his lips a mere light, brushing caress on her mouth. "Most women don't achieve anything close to their peak the first time."

"And I did," she said smugly.

He laughed, falling back onto the bed beside her. "Yes, my sweet, I believe you did. But I believe you have higher peaks yet to summit."

"Oh?" She turned on her side, propping her cheek on her palm, her eyes bright with exhilaration. "Why is that?"

"Because no one can do everything they're capable of first time around," he stated, sitting up. He swung himself off the bed and went to the washstand. He poured water into the basin, dipped a cloth into it, and came back to her. "This might be a little cold, but you will feel more comfortable." Bending over her, he sponged her belly and the tops of her thighs and then matter-of-factly moved her legs apart and cleansed the blood from her inner thighs. "You may be a little sore in the morning, but it will pass."

He tossed the cloth back into the basin and with a swift movement lifted her off the bed long enough to pull down the coverlet and insert her between the sheets. "Better?"

"Mm." A delicious languor was creeping over her as she sank into the deep feather mattress. "Will you stay?"

"I dare not. We must be up betimes for the hunt, and we both need to sleep." He dressed quickly, leaving his shirt unbuttoned, and then came back to the bed, kissing her forehead. "Sweet dreams, Harry."

She smiled sleepily up at him. "You didn't kill Nick."

He paused for an instant, and the shadows crossed his eyes again. "No, I didn't kill Nick . . . but I was responsible for his death." And then he was gone, the door clicking shut behind him.

Harriet sat up, her languor vanished. What did he mean? He was *responsible*? How could he have been responsible? How *could* he say something like that and then just leave her? The dream world was gone now, and everything she had seen that evening flooded back in a cold wash of bitter reality. She *had* seen the man who had just loved her meeting in the woods with a foreign agent.

She scrambled out of bed, grabbing her nightgown, dragging it over her head. She let herself out of her chamber and ran down the silent corridor to the landing and into the wing that housed the guest apartments. She flung open his door as violently as he had flung open hers what now seemed a lifetime ago.

"What do you mean?" she demanded. "How were you responsible?"

Julius, still in his britches, shirt hanging open, turned from the dresser where he was pouring himself cognac. He sighed wearily. "Can we talk of this tomorrow, Harriet? Now is not the time, and you need your sleep."

"*Sleep!*" she exclaimed. "How could I possibly sleep when you say something like that? After what we've just done together . . . What did you mean?" She almost stamped her bare foot in frustration.

Julius cursed his impulse. He had regretted the words the moment they came out of his mouth, but her openness, the honesty of her response to him in her bedchamber, had affected him so deeply that he had spoken the truth without thought. He owed her his own honesty. But that had been a foolish, sentimental mistake. He searched for words that would minimize the damage, but under the burning question in those candid green eyes, he could find nothing.

He shook his head. "Because of my actions, Harriet, Nick was unable to defend himself from a sudden attack."

"What actions?" She was calmer now but watchful.

He debated for a moment and then asked, "How much do you know of what your brother did?"

"I know he was a spy for England. He told me so himself. I know he was murdered somewhere on the Continent, presumably by French agents. The Ministry told me that. So where were you?" Her heart was beating too rapidly again, as if she stood on the brink of an as yet unknown danger. But she would not back down . . . not now, not after what they had done together. "Where were *you*?" she repeated with more emphasis.

His expression was bleak, his voice expressionless, the words emerging in a staccato rhythm. "I was there, but I could do nothing for him. I had a mission to accomplish, and Nick could not be part of it. Sometimes I had to work alone. I had put something in his drink to send him to sleep for a few hours, but it meant that when he was attacked, he couldn't focus enough to defend himself properly." He turned away from her then, raising the glass to his lips, draining its contents in one swallow.

"If you were there, why could you not help him?" she pressed, nausea rising in her throat.

He sighed again, a weary, almost defeated sound. "Because I had my own mission to accomplish, and I could not jeopardize it with any delay. Too many other lives depended on it. I had to choose between one and the many."

She stared at his averted back, swallowing the nausea, tasting the acid bile at the back of her throat. "So you are a double agent, working for the French." It was a flat statement.

He spun round on her, and anger now flickered anew in his dark gaze. "Do you really think that, Harriet?" He shook his head at her, waving his hand in a gesture of dismissal. "You disappoint me."

"*I* disappoint *you*," she breathed in shock and outrage. He had no right to turn the tables like that. With an incoherent sound, she left him standing there, her bare feet racing away from him as if she were pursued by the Furies.

Once in her own chamber again, she closed the door and stood leaning against it, unaware for the moment that tears were spilling down her cheeks. After the tumultuous emotions of the evening, she could not think clearly about anything. She was aware only of a deep and desperate sense of betrayal, and Nick's loss was suddenly as raw and immediate as it had been when she had first faced it. *Julius could have saved him. He didn't have to die.*

Cold now, she crawled back under the covers, seeking the warmth she had left a few minutes earlier, but she could find no comfort, nothing to stop the shaking that convulsed her limbs.

Chapter Twelve

Harriet must have fallen asleep eventually, because when she opened her eyes again, it was to the sound of Agnes drawing back the curtains.

"Good morning, my lady. Did you sleep well?" The maid set the tray of hot chocolate and bread and butter on the bed as Harriet dragged herself up against the pillows.

"Yes, thank you," Harriet fibbed, aware that her eyes still felt swollen from weeping. They must look awful, she thought. But Agnes did not look exactly bright-eyed, either, this morning. The servants' ball must have gone on late into the night and Mallow's Christmas punch was renowned for its punch.

"Your riding boots are scuffed and muddy, my

lady." Agnes held up the boots Harriet had been wearing in the woods the previous night. "I'll take them downstairs for the boot boy to shine." She cast a curious glance at her mistress. "I was sure I'd seen that they were clean before I went off last evening, m'lady."

"I went for a walk," Harriet said. "I felt a little restless, and it was a fine night, so I took a stroll around the garden."

"Oh, right y'are, m'lady." Agnes hurried away with the boots, and Harriet sat back against the pillow, sipping her chocolate.

The events of the night were as vivid this morning as they had been while she was living them. They hadn't left her even during her intermittent dozing, and she felt only an overwhelming desire to lock her door, curl up under the covers again, and sleep until Twelfth Night had come and gone and the house was finally empty once more. Surely Julius would have the decency to leave as soon as he could? She knew who he was, knew *what* he was. He couldn't continue to abuse her grandfather's hospitality. She decided that if he hadn't left before the hunt began, she would tell the Duke everything. Then he would have to go. There would be no mail carrier on Boxing Day, but tomorrow she would send a message to the Ministry in London, and her task would be over.

She set the tray aside and slid out of bed, wincing a little as she took a step to the washstand, where Agnes had left a steaming pitcher of hot water. Her legs shook, and she grabbed the post at the foot of the bed, physical memory of the previous night flooding her, making her toes curl into the Aubusson carpet. She could hear Julius's voice telling her she would probably be a little sore today, feel his hands on her again as he sponged gently between her thighs.

She clung to the bedpost until the moment passed and then took a deep breath. What had happened was real. She was no longer virgin, and that in itself was all to the good, she decided with characteristic honesty. It was a burden she was well rid of. She had no suitors, no young men pressing her for her favor. She spent most of her time in town depressing such pretensions as gently but as directly as she could. And while she was quite prepared to go to her grave a spinster, she was very glad that it would not be as a virginal spinster.

For that, she had to thank Julius Forsythe. The man who had stood by and watched her brother die.

The reflection was sufficient to wipe away whatever satisfaction she was feeling. She wanted a bath, but there was no time before breakfast. It would have to be later, after the hunt. She pulled the nightgown over her head and walked gingerly to the washstand, pouring steaming water into the basin. A cake of verbena-scented soap and a washcloth brought a degree of soothing comfort to her body, and a pad of witch hazel on her swollen eyes restored her complexion to something approaching its usual composure.

Agnes came in with her newly polished boots. "Nurse Maddox says she'll try to keep the children in the nursery until after breakfast, my lady. But they're very excited."

It was a welcome change to turn her attention to familiar problems. "I'm sure they are, Agnes, but if anyone can keep them in check, it's Nurse Maddox." Harriet turned from the washstand and began to dress as the maid handed her undergarments to her. She slipped her arms into the sleeves of the crisply starched white shirt with its high lace collar and pulled on the leather britches she wore beneath her tawny orange riding skirt. She stepped into the skirt, tucking the shirt into the waistband before Agnes fastened the buttons at her back. A black silk waistcoat over the shirt and a fitted jacket of the same color as the skirt completed the outfit. Agnes took a soft brush and smoothed over the black velvet collar and cuffs of the coat.

" 'Tis very elegant, m'lady," the girl said, with a mixture of pleasure and pride in her own handiwork.

"It won't be when I get back," Harriet said with a rueful smile as she sat down to pull on her boots. "If the hunt takes its usual course, I'll be covered in mud from head to toe by the time we get home."

"You'll be in the front, then, m'lady?" Agnes regarded her with a degree of awe.

She nodded. She and Nick had always competed to keep up with the Master and the Huntsman, and he was going to be with her in spirit on this Boxing Day hunt, she had decided long since. Judd would take over the children after a couple of hours when they tired, as they would, however much they protested. And then she would be free to give herself and her horse their heads.

There was no way Julius Forsythe would be joining this hunt.

She walked down to the hall, nodded at the footman, and went into the dining salon, where those intent on hunting were gathering for an early breakfast. She stopped on the threshold. The Earl of Marbury, in riding dress, was standing at the sideboard, a plate in his hand, talking to the Duke, as relaxed as he always had been in this house. The two men turned to her as she paused in the doorway, and the Duke, in hunting pink as befitted the Master of Hounds, waved her over.

"Good morning, my dear. I hope you're well rested for today's exertions."

Her eyes involuntarily went to the Earl, who merely bowed. "Good morning, Lady Harriet."

"Sir." She sketched a curtsy and then turned deliberately to her grandfather. "Do you know which covert Jackson intends to draw first, Duke?"

"Carlton Woods, I believe," the Duke said. "Eat, my dear." He waved expansively to the dishes arrayed on the sideboard. "Hunting's hungry work." He carried his own laden plate to the table.

"How could you still be here?" Harriet hissed in an undertone. "You are a traitor, you're betraying my family . . . If you do not leave immediately, I shall tell my grandfather everything I know."

To her astonishment, he just smiled. "I think you will find there is nothing you can tell him, my dear. But regardless, I am here for the children. I made them a solemn promise that I would ride with them this morning. Would you have me renege on that promise?"

"I imagine that is something you do on a regular basis, sir. The children will recover. They have come through worse." She turned her back on him under the pretext of examining the covered dishes on the sideboard.

"There is no need for this, Harriet." He took her plate from her and forked a slice of ham onto it.

"How could you possibly say that? You're a double agent, using my family's house to betray your country," she accused in a furious undertone. "You expect me to smile and behave as if I don't know that?"

"Yes," he said bluntly. "Because you don't. Now, be careful." He shot a warning glance at the room behind her before saying casually, "Do you care for eggs, ma'am?"

They were surrounded by people, the buzz of conversation rising and falling in the room. But he was right, they were conspicuous, and Harriet was conscious of the glances coming their way. "Thank you, no." She took the plate from him and went to find a seat at the table. What did he mean about there being nothing she could tell the Duke? She could tell him everything . . . expose Julius Forsythe for the traitor he was.

Julius stood looking at her rather absently for a moment, wishing they were anywhere but there. There was nothing he could do in this crowd to put things right between them. It would have to wait.

The baying of the hounds on the gravel sweep at the front of the house brought breakfast to a swift end. Harriet went into the hall just as the children came hurtling down the stairs. "They're here, Harry! The hounds are here!"

"Yes, I know, I can hear them myself," she said calmly. "Stand still a minute. Gracie, your stock is all twisted now." She retied the white cravat at the little girl's neck and then turned to examine Tom. He stood very still and straight, his head high over his own starched cravat. "You'll do," she said with a smile, thinking how much he resembled Nick at that moment.

"Where's the Earl?" Tom demanded. "He promised we'd ride up with him."

"He's here, and he will keep his promise," Julius said from behind Harriet. He held his gloves in one hand, his hat in the other, and his whip under his arm.

The children greeted him with shrieks of delight, and Harriet was left on the sidelines as they dragged him to the front door. The grooms were bringing the horses from the stables, and the red-coated Huntsman and his fellows were mounted, the baying hounds swirling at the feet of the impatient horses, the whippers-in moving among the dogs, keeping them in some semblance of order.

Judd held the children's ponies to one side of the melee. A groom held Harriet's own chestnut mare which was sidling alongside Julius's gray gelding, rolling her eyes at the other horse.

Harriet had the absurd thought that her own Ladybird was flirting with Julius's aptly named Casanova, and an involuntary laugh came to her lips. She felt rather than saw Julius's quick, questioning glance at her and sobered instantly, calming her horse with her hand on the mare's neck. The groom bent to offer his palm for her waiting foot and tossed her up into the saddle. She adjusted her position, her leg angled over the side pommel, aware of a faint residual soreness as she moved in the saddle.

Judd had both children mounted and was astride his own sturdy cob, the ponies' reins still securely held in his own hand.

"Judd's not going to lead us, is he, Harry?" the children chorused. "*Harry,* he mustn't. He can't."

"No, no, he's not," Harriet reassured them. "But he needs to keep the ponies back until the Huntsman and the Duke have taken the pack out first. We're drawing Carlton Woods first, so it will be an easy canter to start with. You needn't worry about falling behind."

They looked doubtful, but fortunately, there was little they could do to take matters into their own hands. Footmen were moving among the horses with trays bearing silver stirrup cups of port for the riders. When he reached Julius, one of the footmen held up his tray on his flat palm.

"Thank you." Julius leaned from the saddle to take the cup.

"This was left for you, my lord." The footman handed him a folded paper and then turned to move off. As he did so, Tom swooped down and reached to take a cup off the tray. Julius intervened swiftly. "That is *not* for you, young Tom. And I'm sure you know it."

Tom flushed guiltily. "I just wanted to try it."

"So did I," his sister said stoutly, not to be outdone.

"Well, you aren't going to." Harriet spoke up.

"And if you give Judd any trouble, he'll bring you straight home. Do you understand?"

Her tone was unusually harsh, and they looked at her in surprised discomfort. Harriet never threatened them.

"Your sister asked you a question," Julius said quietly. "It would be polite to answer. Do you understand what she said?"

They both nodded, chastened. Judd gave the Earl a nod of approval, but Julius didn't notice. He frowned at the paper he'd just unfolded. The message was short and to the point. He folded it up again and tucked it inside his coat. What could be so urgent that Marcel needed to meet him this morning? The rendezvous would be easy enough to reach during the hunt, and he could slip away without difficulty. The hunting field was notoriously chaotic, but nevertheless, it was most unusual to call for a meeting in public and in full daylight.

The Huntsman blew his horn, and the horses and dogs moved down the driveway, the hunters falling in behind the Master until they had crossed the narrow lane at the end of the long driveway and into the first stretch of fields.

Harriet was torn. She did not want to ride with

Julius, but she couldn't leave the children, and it seemed he was going to honor his promise. They kept in the middle of the field of hunters, and the children quickly forgot their discomfiture, cantering between Harriet and Julius. A small ditch brought triumphant cries of exhilaration from them as they jumped it, and Harriet forgot for a second who was riding alongside her and turned to exchange a grin with Julius. He returned it, and she fought angrily with herself for a moment. *God damn the man.* For one betraying moment, she had thought she was sharing that private moment with Nick. And Julius hadn't had the decency to realize it, to pretend he hadn't seen her smile.

Grimly, she set her sights on the first covert.

Julius rode for the most part in silence, keeping a close eye on the twins as they entered the wood. The hunt was packed closely together at this early stage of the morning, and their ponies were restless, but they seemed capable enough of controlling them. And Judd was there, watchful and ready to intervene. Julius relaxed his vigil and allowed his horse to fall back a little. He glanced at Harriet. Her profile was set, that pointed chin at a grim angle.

What in the devil's name had happened to him? He knew he could not lie to her, but he deeply regretted saying anything to her about her brother's death. Keeping secrets had never been a problem for him; his life depended upon it. He hadn't been forced to tell her the whole truth. He could have left her with the part he'd given her, that he had not personally killed Nick.

And yet he had not been able to help himself. For the first time that he could remember, his heart had ruled his head. He wanted to be with her, to make love with her, to learn her through and through, to discover every little thing about her, and he could not do that if she did not know the truth, know it and understand it. She had to understand him as he understood her. She had to know what made him the person he was, why he did what he did. And never before had he felt like that about anyone. So what did that mean?

But it was a rhetorical question. He knew the answer even if he had not acknowledged it. He loved Harriet Devere. And he had never expected to love anyone in that way, never expected to allow anyone to get that close to him, to get inside him the way she was. It had happened imperceptibly, as he'd become acutely conscious of her presence, as he'd watched her, entranced by her laughter, her smile, the little gesture she made with her shoulders, the ready wit, the glorious sensuality of her body. It had crept up on him until suddenly the truth had burst upon him, what the French so aptly called *un coup de foudre.* But what the hell was he to do about it? By revealing himself to her, it seemed that he had destroyed any feelings she might have held for him . . . any feelings she *could* have for him.

Harriet felt his gaze. It was like a magnet drawing her towards him, forcing her to acknowledge him. Slowly and against her will, she turned her head to meet the intensity in the black eyes. He mouthed, "Trust me. Please."

Why should she trust him? He was a traitor; his life was based upon lies. And yet . . . and yet there was nothing Harriet wanted to do more. Her soul yearned to trust him, to give herself to him again, as whole-heartedly as she had done the night before.

She turned her head away from his gaze in a sharp negative. *No. I cannot.*

Chapter Thirteen

He had a lot of work to do, Julius thought grimly. And he was going to need some help. The Huntsman's horn shattered the tense silence, and the children, riding just ahead, shrieked with excitement. The hunt sprang into life, riders urging their mounts into a gallop. Hooves thundered through the wood, horses jostling for position. The horn sounded again, and the hounds in full cry raced for the clear ground opening ahead through the trees.

"Come on, then." Julius brought Casanova up with the children. "Give them their heads. I'm right beside you." They needed no further encouragement, and the ponies surged forward, Julius keeping an easy pace beside them. Harriet caught up with them as they emerged from the wood, still positioned in the middle of the hunt.

"This way," she called, gesturing with her whip to the side. "We'll take the gate over there instead of the hedge. It'll put us ahead of the field. I'll give you a lead." She turned Ladybird away from the jostling riders heading for the hedge and galloped to the gate. Julius followed, the children's ponies on Casanova's heels, Judd on his sturdy cob keeping up the rear.

Harriet was already opening the gate as they reached her. "Hurry," she instructed, drawing Ladybird to one side so that they could precede her through the gate.

"I wish we could have jumped the hedge." Tom looked longingly at the line of riders leaping the hedge.

"It's too high for your ponies," Harriet told him. "There's a lower one across the next field. You can take that."

"I'll take Tom, you take Grace," Julius said briskly. "We'll meet in the far field." Tom, with a whoop of glee, nudged his pony into a gallop behind Julius.

"Come on, then, Gracie, let's beat them to it." Harriet and Nick had always had friendly races to the next obstacle, and she was suddenly determined not to be outdone by the Earl. She touched her horse lightly with her whip, and the mare leaped forward. Grace set her pony to follow, and they rode for the hedge. They were in the front of the field now, and Harriet felt the familiar surge of exhilaration. Catching the fox was the least important aspect of hunting; it was the wild ride of a long run that she loved, the sound of beating hooves in her ears, the whistle of the wind as she bent lower over her mare's neck, encouraging her to greater speed.

Casanova was half a head in front of Ladybird as they approached the hedge. Mentally consigning the twins to Judd's care, Harriet put the mare to the jump and sailed over a bare inch ahead of the gelding. She drew rein on the other side, panting slightly, laughing, her hair, escaping the confines of its braid, wisped out from beneath her plumed hat.

Julius drew rein beside her just as the children's ponies came over the hedge. They landed neatly, Tom a shade ahead of his sister. "Bravo." Julius congratulated them. "That was nicely done, both of you."

Judd's cob landed beside them. "I reckon another hour'll do them, Lady Harriet."

"Yes, of course," Harriet agreed, ignoring the chorus of protests from the twins. They would be tired enough in an hour to go home with only a minimum of fuss. They'd still have a two-hour ride ahead of them and would be exhausted by the time they reached the nursery.

Julius glanced up at the weak sun. It would be about ten o'clock, he reckoned. Marcel would be waiting for him in the spinney at half past eleven. The hunt had come to a halt. The hounds had lost the scent of the fox and were now circling and baying at the far end of the field, while the Master and the Huntsman conferred.

"Where will they draw next?" Julius asked.

"I don't know. Probably Hobson's Thicket," Harriet returned. "They usually go there from here. What d'you think, Judd?"

"Aye, that'll be next," Judd agreed in his phlegmatic fashion.

They trotted across the field to catch up with the main body of the hunt. Julius had ridden this land many times with Nick and knew the ground almost as well as he did the countryside around his own home. His rendezvous with Marcel in the spinney was about half a mile from Hobson's Thicket, he calculated. He would stay with them until the next covert had been drawn, and once the children had gone home, he would find a way to detach himself. He didn't think

Harriet, in her present frame of mind, would attempt to keep him at her side.

They drew a blank at the next covert but had a good run to the third, where the children, protesting, were sent back with Judd. Harriet watched them go and then, without a word to Julius, rode up to her grandfather, who was in conference again with Jackson.

"Ah, there you are, Harriet." The Duke greeted her. "Having a good morning, although the devil's in the scent today. Jackson thinks the ground's too hard for it to stay around long enough."

"The runs are good, though," she returned with a quick smile at the Huntsman. "The children have gone back with Judd."

The Duke nodded absently. "So, on to Mill Bottom Field, Jackson?"

"Aye, your grace. We often find there."

Harriet glanced around. Julius had not accompanied her across the field. She hadn't invited him to, of course, but she was surprised nevertheless. No, more disconcerted, she amended with characteristic honesty. She could see no sign of him in the shifting throng of horses and riders. Her grandfather and

Jackson were leading the hunt on to the next covert, and she had turned her horse to join the parade when something caught her eye. Looking over her shoulder to the rear of the bunched crowd, she saw the raw-boned gray gelding picking his way around the edge of the field.

Where was he going? It was the wrong direction for home, but it was definitely away from the hunt. She let the crowd surround her and move on. Lady-bird shifted uncertainly, whickering at the departing horses. With sudden resolution, Harriet pulled the reins and turned the mare away from the hunt, nudging her in the direction of the departing Julius. He disappeared through a gap in the hedge, and she set her horse to follow. Why, she didn't know. She had wanted to be rid of him for good, and instead, she was following him. Maybe he would give her more evidence for his treachery, although she had more than enough to satisfy the men at the Ministry. But something spurred her on.

She went through the same gap in the hedge and saw him now at the far side of the paddock, heading for a small but dense crop of trees. Bluebell Spinney. So called for obvious reasons, but outside the early spring, it was as nondescript a place as one could imagine. She hung back, not wanting him to know she was following. Not that it would make much difference to anything now, she reflected dourly.

He disappeared into the trees, and she trotted Ladybird across the paddock. Some distance behind her, she could hear the Huntsman's horn as the hounds found again. Ladybird whickered, sniffing the air. She was a hunter born and bred, and riding away from that sound went against every instinct. Harriet soothed her with a pat on her neck and rode her forward. At the edge of the spinney, she drew rein, listening. There was an odd silence in the air, not even the cawing of a rook. And there were plenty of them nesting high up in the trees. And then she heard it. The clash of steel upon steel, ringing faintly from somewhere within the spinney.

Harriet nudged the mare forward, entering the dim shadows beneath the trees. The ring of steel was louder, but there were no voices, no other sounds at all. She followed what she could hear. The shadowy gloom lightened ahead of her, where she knew there was a clearing, which in spring was carpeted with bluebells. She dismounted and cautiously led Ladybird forward. Whatever was going on in the clearing, her sudden arrival could not be welcome.

The space between the trees grew wider, and she moved sideways into the shadows again as the clearing came into view. What she saw stopped her heart in her throat. Julius, still mounted, was fighting two men on the ground, men with swords and daggers who were slashing upwards at him. Casanova was bleeding from a wound on his flank, but he caracoled around the clearing, hooves flailing, as powerful a weapon as the wicked blade in Julius's hand. But it was only a matter of time, Harriet thought, before one of those daggers brought Casanova crashing to the ground. And when that happened—

She didn't finish the thought, swinging back onto the mare. Raising her crop high in the air, she kicked Ladybird's flanks, and the horse sprang forward, startled at such an unusual spur. Her lips were pulled back, revealing the strong yellow teeth that could bite a chunk out of a man. Harriet drew back on the reins, bringing the mare onto her hind legs, and her front hooves flailed, catching one of Julius's assailants on the shoulder, sending him reeling to the ground. Using her crop, Harriet leaned low over the mare's neck and slashed at the man who was still on his feet. The sudden violence of her appearance had thrown the assailants off balance, and Julius's blade flashed, a silver streak in the wintery light. The man on his feet jumped back with a cry, his hand pressed to his side. His companion was up again now, though, and Harriet rode at him again. She thought it was the slight Frenchman from the previous night, Julius's contact in the French network. Why were they attacking him?

But the question seemed immaterial. Ladybird whinnied frantically as a dagger came perilously close to her neck, and Harriet slashed wildly at the man with her crop. It caught him across the cheek, and a line of blood sprang forth. She did it again and again, some part of her mind astonished at the ferocity of which she was capable.

The Frenchman fell back from the assault, blood pouring from his face. One arm hung at an odd angle against his side. Ladybird's hoof must have dislocated his shoulder, Harriet thought distantly. She hauled back on the reins again, and the mare reared again, teeth bared, and knocked him to the ground once more. This time, he did not get up.

Harriet turned to see what Julius was doing and was just in time to see his sword slip soundlessly through his assailant's chest. The man crumpled to the ground. Julius sprang from his horse and swiftly examined the man, drawing his sword free in a gush of blood. He went over to the other one, who lay on the ground, clutching his shoulder.

"Look the other way," Julius ordered Harriet in a cold, hard voice, and she obeyed without hesitation. She could guess what he was going to do. And after her own mad frenzy, she knew that she was probably capable of doing the same in the right circumstances.

"All right?" His voice was suddenly very close to her, and she turned her ashen countenance towards him. He stood at her stirrup and placed a hand on her knee. "I owe you my life." It was a quiet statement. "Fool that I am, I was not expecting an ambush." There was a note of bitterness in his voice now.

"Who are they?" Harriet kept her eyes averted from the inert shapes on the ground.

"French agents. Somehow I must have made a mistake. I thought my cover was unbreakable . . . not so, it would seem." He glanced over to his erstwhile assailants, his mouth twisted.

She stared at him, bemused. Her blood was still flowing fast with the violent exertions of the last few minutes, and her mind grasped for something that would make sense of it all. "You're not a double agent?"

He shook his head. "No, my dear, I am *not* a double

agent. Our friends, however, were supposed to believe that I was. And, indeed, did so most satisfactorily for many months. I don't know what alerted them . . . but I will find out."

"But why . . . why did the Ministry believe that you were a double agent? They told me to get evidence against you."

He gave her a wry smile. "Yes, I rather thought so. But I wasn't certain until I found you in the woods last night."

"You didn't find me," she protested. "You didn't see me."

"I knew you were there, though. Why do you think I locked the door?"

"Maybe so, but still, why did the Ministry believe you were a traitor?"

"I wasn't ready to tell them what I was doing. Not yet. I was working for myself, without the knowledge of the powers that be, and that, my dear, is forbidden in the agency." He pushed a hand through his hair, his expression suddenly clearing. "I was too damned sure of myself, too damned arrogant to ask for help. But I did what had to be done in the end." He swept a hand around the clearing in an all-encompassing gesture.

"Killing them, you mean?" She frowned, bemused. "You needed to kill them for your own reasons."

"I killed them for Nick," he stated without expression. "People who kill my friends do not stay alive."

"They killed Nick?" Some glimmer of enlightenment shone in her befuddled brain.

"Yes," he said shortly. "And they were about to kill me, if it hadn't been for your timely arrival."

"What do we do with them now?" Harriet asked, astounded at how her mind seemed able to absorb everything she'd just heard, everything she'd seen and done herself, and move on to practicalities as if it were all the most natural business in the world. Perhaps the shock would come later. Or perhaps she was following in her father's footsteps as naturally as her brother had done.

"Nothing," Julius stated. "Someone will find their bodies soon enough, and it will look as if they killed each other. No one's going to investigate the deaths of a couple of foreigners, particularly Frenchmen, when we're at war with them." He took her reins and led Ladybird to where Casanova stood still, head hanging, at the side of the clearing. The gash on his flank oozed sluggishly. Julius examined it carefully and swore under his breath.

"How bad is it?"

"Not as bad as it might be," he returned, "but I need to get it attended to quickly."

"Judd will do that. He's a miracle worker with horses."

"That does not surprise me," Julius said drily. He went to the gelding's head and spoke to him softly, then took the reins. "Will your mare take us both, do you think? I don't want to open that gash any further."

"She's tired, but she's strong." She inched forward on the saddle as he swung up behind her, reaching around her for the mare's reins, holding them loosely in one hand, his other holding those of the gelding walking docilely alongside Ladybird.

"Lean back against me. I want to feel you close." It was another matter-of-fact statement, and yet it sent a jolt through her loins. She could feel the hard lines of his body against her back, the warm security of his arms encircling her, smell the musky scent of his sweat mingling with her own.

"Will you trust me, Harriet?" He spoke against her ear as he guided both horses away from the blood-stained clearing.

"Yes," she said softly. "But you must trust me, too. You must trust me to keep your secrets."

"I do trust you and will trust you with those secrets I am empowered to share," he said.

A little shiver ran down her spine. "There will be some you cannot share with me?"

"Those that are given me by others, yes."

It felt as if they were negotiating some kind of contract, she thought. But what kind?

As if he heard her unspoken question, Julius asked softly, "I want to marry you, Harry. Even knowing what you do about me, could you spend the rest of your life with me?"

"I hadn't thought to marry anyone," she murmured, and was disconcerted to feel him laugh behind her.

"I do love your honesty, my sweet Harriet. What you mean to say, though, is that you have not—*had* not, I hope—met anyone you could imagine as your husband." He nuzzled her neck, and she felt his breath warm on her skin. "Will you answer me now?"

Of course she would marry him. There was no question in her mind. She had never been able to imagine the kind of man she would be happy to share her life with, but she knew he would have to be someone out of the usual run. Someone just like Julius Forsythe, who promised a life of excitement and upheaval and the deepest loving commitment. He felt for her what she felt for him, it was as simple as that. There would be fireworks, of course. What kind of marriage could exist without them? Julius was strong . . . and tyrannical? Quite possibly. He was accustomed to having his own way. But then, so was she.

"I'm waiting, Harry," he murmured behind her.

She leaned back against him, letting her head rest for a moment in the crook of his shoulder. "Yes, of course I'll marry you . . . and it will certainly suit the children. They'll be over the moon," she added.

"Harriet." He squeezed her hard. "Let's get one thing straight. You will not marry me for the sake of the children. It's past time you stopped living your life only according to what's good for them. Yes, I will be an elder brother to them. I will look after them and welcome them under my roof. But I am not marrying them. It's you I want. And only you. Is that clear?"

"Oh, yes, indeed, my lord. Very clear," she responded with a mock docility that made him laugh. "However, you must gain my grandfather's permission. Have you thought of that?"

"I don't think that will be an insuperable obstacle."

"He has to know about you." All mockery had left her. She stared straight ahead, drawing herself upright away from him. "I cannot marry you if my grandfather does not know the truth about you, and about Nick, and about your part in his death." She didn't know why she was making this condition, and yet she knew it was right. This marriage could not begin in a morass of deception. The Duke had to know.

"My dear girl, the Duke knows everything," Julius said, pulling her back into his embrace. "He has always known."

Harriet had not thought anything could surprise her again, but she'd been mistaken. "How?" She twisted her head around to look at him.

"Your father . . . Nick . . . they were both following in the Duke's footsteps. Spying is a Devere family business, my sweet. That's why you were recruited. Your grandfather suggested you as the obvious choice to receive Nick's encrypted messages. You weren't supposed to get any more deeply involved in the business, and I daresay there will be some very uncomfortable folk at the Ministry when your grandfather has had his say."

Harriet's mind was reeling. And yet through the confusion, she could catch at some threads of sense.

It certainly explained the attachment between her grandfather and Julius. "Does he truly know everything about your part in Nick's death?"

"Yes. And he knows that I did only what he would have done—what Nick would have done—in the same circumstances. We honor our vows in the service, Harriet. And you will be expected to honor them, too."

A family business, Harriet thought. And her grandfather had been prepared to lose first his son and then his grandson in his country's service. The world no longer seemed the one she thought she knew. She could find nothing to say and was thankful that Julius seemed, for the moment at least, to accept her silence. They were approaching Charlbury Hall from the rear and took the horses straight into the stables. Judd was in the yard, giving instructions to a groom about the children's ponies, but he came over to them instantly.

"Eh, what 'appened to you, then, lad?" He examined Casanova's injured flank. "Nasty cut, that."

"A bramble caught him, Judd," Julius said calmly, dismounting. "It will need cleansing, salve—"

"I know my own business, m'lord," Judd stated

firmly, giving his lordship a steady stare from beneath bushy gray eyebrows.

"Yes, of course you do. Forgive me." Julius gave him a ruefully apologetic smile. One did not give instructions to Judd when it came to horseflesh. The man also knew a knife cut when he saw one, and he'd been in the Duke's service for long enough to know rather more than that.

Julius turned back to Ladybird and lifted Harriet from the saddle. He held her in the air for a moment, looking a question into her eyes.

Infinitesimally, she nodded, and he set her down. "You need a bath, my love. And so do I. Can it be arranged?"

"Together?" Her eyes widened as she thought of managing such a thing in the early afternoon among the great-aunts.

"Can you think of a pleasanter way?" he asked, a teasing glint in his eye.

"No," she said frankly, and her eyes began to dance at such an outrageous prospect. "Come to my chamber in half an hour. But don't let anyone see you." She handed the mare's reins to the groom, who had come running to take the horse to the stables.

"As if I would . . . give me some credit, Harry," Julius returned. "This is my business, if you remember."

"All too vividly," she replied, and walked away, surprised at how much energy she seemed to have despite the extraordinary rigors of the morning.

Chapter Fourteen

Harriet lay back in the deep hip bath before a blazing fire in her chamber, languidly passing a cake of soap over her body beneath the water. She heard the faint click of the door beyond the screen, and her body quickened with anticipation. She closed her eyes and waited.

"A veritable Aphrodite," his voice murmured above her. "Draw your knees up, and give me some room."

She opened her eyes. He was standing gloriously naked, gloriously aroused, at the foot of the bath. Obligingly, she drew her knees closer to her body, and he stepped into the water, sliding down, sending a wash of water over the edge onto the sheets that surrounded the bath. "You'll cause a flood," she protested faintly as he pushed his feet beneath her backside.

"It'll dry," he responded with a careless smile. His toes wriggled intimately beneath her, and she inhaled sharply. He leaned forward and took her nipples between finger and thumb, rolling them delicately. "Where's the soap?"

Wordlessly, she handed it to him, and he began to soap her breasts before moving down over her belly beneath the water. He drew the soap down the backs of her thighs, and her muscles tightened with anticipation. He watched her face, a slight smile on his lips, as he brought his hand closer and closer to her core, exposed by her drawn-up knees. He kept her waiting, tantalizing her with little forays along the insides of her thighs even as his toes continued their intimate teasing.

"This isn't fair," she whispered.

"All's fair in love and war," he returned softly, still watching her expression. "I'll know when it's time, my sweet."

It was the most delicious torment, almost unendurable to be so close that she knew the slightest brush of his hand on her sex would send her over the top, and at last his fingers found her. Her body jumped at the light, delicate touch, a mere lick of a fingertip on the hard nub of flesh, and wave after wave of glorious sensation rippled through her.

Julius leaned forward and kissed her. "How lovely you look. Do you have any idea what pleasure it gives me to see you transported like that?"

Her eyes opened slowly. "That was different," she said on a note of wonder. "Not the same as last night."

"There are many variations on this theme, sweetheart." He sat back, smiling at her. "I can't wait to introduce you to them all." He reached for her hands and pulled her forward until she was straddling his thighs. "Let us try one more. Lift up a little."

Willingly, she lifted herself a few inches and then gasped as she felt him enter her from below. Slowly, she sank back onto his thighs, feeling his presence deep within her. "You control this now," he said. "Move as you wish, find what gives you the most pleasure."

She caught her bottom lip between her teeth, concentrating on sensation. The feel and movement of the water added another dimension to the whole delightful business. She looked into his eyes, watching as they grew smoky with his own pleasure, and once again, she was aware of that heady sense of power. Instinctively, she circled her body around him, feeling the throb of his penis within her. A tiny sound came from him, and for a moment his eyes closed. She circled the other way, felt his thighs tighten beneath her backside as he thrust his hips upwards. The orgasmic tide this time was a surge, a flood of exquisite sensation.

Julius pulled her head down into his shoulder, stifling her exultant cries, and only when the wave receded did Harriet hear the sounds beyond the locked chamber door. Voices, footsteps—the hunt was returning. There were people in the corridors, servants hurrying with jugs of hot bathwater.

"How are you going to get out?" she whispered on a bubble of laughter. "There are people everywhere."

"I'll just have to stay here," he said equably, reaching sideways to flick a towel off the screen. He stood up in a shower of water, and she looked at him with a knowing smile. His penis was curled into its damp nest of curls, spent and satisfied. And she was responsible for that satisfaction. "Have you seen enough, ma'am?" he asked with a grin, holding the towel away from his body.

"For the moment," she returned, her eyes narrowing.

He wrapped the towel around his loins and took

another off the screen, holding it open for her. "Come, then."

Harriet stepped out of the bath, and he wrapped the towel around her. "Agnes will come knocking in a moment," she said, moving the fire screen aside. "What are we going to do?" Her eyes were alight with laughter, although there was nothing really amusing about their predicament.

Julius shrugged into his dressing robe as he went to the window. He opened it and looked down. "Not much to hold on to there."

"No. Anyway, you couldn't possibly climb down the wisteria in a dressing gown!" she exclaimed.

"Then we must do this the boring way," he said with a mock sigh. "Ring for your maid. I'll stand behind the door, and when she comes in, I will slip out."

"You sound as if you've done this before." Harriet pulled the bell rope vigorously. "Do you make a habit of escaping from ladies' bedchambers?"

"Not exactly a habit of it," he responded with a judicious nod that sent her into a peal of laughter again. "When I'm dressed, I shall go to the Duke. The sooner we make this legitimate, the sooner we can stop all this creeping around."

Harriet nodded, and he slipped behind the door to await Agnes.

An hour later, Harriet was dressed for the evening, fastening a pair of diamond studs in her ears, when there was a knock at her door. Agnes went to answer it.

"His grace would like to see Lady Harriet in the library as soon as she is ready," the footman announced.

"Thank you, Collins." Harriet fastened the second stud and rose from the dresser stool. "I'll be down right away." She hurried after the footman, her heart beating fast with a mixture of apprehension and excitement. There seemed to be a surfeit of both in her life since Julius Forsythe had appeared in it, she reflected. *Will it always be so?*

She went into the library without ceremony. The Duke and the Earl were standing in front of the fire, glasses in hand, and they both turned, smiling, to greet her. Julius came forward quickly and took her hand, raising it to his lips with uncharacteristic formality, before leading her to the fire.

"So, Harriet, I understand you and Julius have

come to an understanding," the Duke said without preamble, handing her a glass of wine.

"Yes, sir." She met his eyes, unflinching, as she took the glass.

He nodded. "Are you sure you understand what life you're entering, my dear? It will not be an easy one."

"My grandmother lived it, as did my mother," she responded.

A slight smile touched his mouth. "True, but they did not know they were living it. You will. You are marrying a man who is devoted to serving his country. That is not a commitment to take lightly."

"I know that," she said, and there was a touch of acerbity in her tone. "I am no fool, Grandfather, and I have no wish to be kept in the dark about anything. This is what I want, and I understand what that means."

He gave her a little bow of acknowledgment. "Then I can only say I wish you every happiness, my dear." He kissed her cheek. "Julius has requested a quick and simple wedding, but I think the family are owed a formal announcement first. I suggest you announce your betrothal at the Feast of the Epiphany. It seems like an appropriate date for many reasons."

Harriet glanced at Julius, who said with a smile, "May I claim the right to make the announcement in my own way, Duke?"

"Certainly," the Duke said. "Are you in agreement, Harriet?"

She nodded. "The Epiphany *does* seem appropriate."

"So let us drink to that." He raised his glass in a toast. "And to you both. May you have many epiphanies. Oh, and just one other thing." His shrewd green eyes held a twinkle of mischief. "Twelfth Night is ten nights hence, a wait that you both might find rather taxing. Whatever you choose to do and wherever you choose to do it in the meantime, I ask only for the utmost discretion, until all of the guests have departed. The great-aunts, you understand . . . ?" The twinkle grew as he sipped his wine, watching them over the lip of his glass.

"Grandfather!" Harriet exclaimed in feigned shock, aware of Julius shaking with laughter beside her. "Is that a carte blanche?"

"I wasn't born yesterday, my dear," he said with a dry smile. "And neither were you. And after the wedding, you will take an extended honeymoon and leave those brats with me and Maddox. We shall manage very well without you. It's past time you thought of yourself first for a change."

"Hear, hear," murmured Julius, raising his glass to the Duke. "We are in your debt, your grace."

Epilogue

TWELFTH NIGHT

"What d'you think'll be in the Twelfth Night cake this year, Tom?" Grace pranced from foot to foot. "It was one of the three kings last year."

"And the baby the year before," Tom said, grimacing as a nursemaid tugged a comb through his tangled hair.

"The best is when it's a gold coin," Grace said. "If it is, and I get it, I'll share it with you, Tom."

"There'll be no coins and no cake if you don't stand still, Lady Grace," Nurse Maddox said through a mouthful of pins as she struggled to fasten up the child's strawberry-blond plait into a becoming circlet around her head.

"Well, at least it won't be a bean," Tom stated with

some satisfaction. "Even though they still call it that. That must have been awful, when all they put in the cake was a bean."

"It did make you king for the night, though," his sister said. "You'd have liked that, telling everyone what to do."

Nurse Maddox clucked her tongue in exasperation. "I don't know what your sister is thinking, letting you stay up until midnight."

"But we always do, Maddox," they chorused. "For years and years we do," Tom added.

"And you're always miserable as sin in the morning," Maddox said. "You'll be staying in bed tomorrow until ten o'clock."

They stared at her, jaws dropping at such an impossibility. "We couldn't. No one can sleep until then," Tom said.

"Oh, you'd be surprised." Maddox stood back to examine her charges. "You'll do. Now, go quietly downstairs, and Mallow will take you into the dining salon."

They set off, trying but failing to keep to a sedate pace. The sounds of music came from the dining salon, a group of local musicians playing from a dais set at the rear of the dining salon for the occasion.

The guests were all seated around the table as the twins entered under Mallow's escort.

Harriet, in a gown of deep crimson velvet opening over a half-slip of silver lace, her grandmother's locket nestling in the hollow of her throat, beckoned to them. She was seated beside Julius at the center of the right side of the table, and the twins scrambled onto empty seats beside her. "We had a nap, Harry," Grace informed her sister righteously. "So you needn't worry about how late it is."

"I wasn't about to," Harriet returned with a smile. "There's lemonade for you."

"When's the cake coming?" Tom looked expectantly to the door.

"Any minute now," his sister reassured. Her mind was not really on the twins for once. Julius had asked to choose his own moment for announcing their betrothal, but the night was almost done, and nothing had been said. He'd been his usual urbane, charming self throughout the evening's festivities, attentive to his fellow guests and in no particular way singling out his about-to-be betrothed. Once or twice, it had been on the tip of her tongue to ask him when he intended to make his announcement, but pride kept her quiet. It was ludicrous, she knew, to appear overeager for something he wanted as much as she did, but some stubborn female instinct kept her mouth shut.

The double doors from the hall opened, and a trumpet blew from the dais as two footmen carried in the enormous circular cake. A gold crown was embedded in the white icing that covered the top.

The twins clapped vigorously, bouncing in their seats as the cake was placed ceremoniously in front of the Duke. It had already been cut into one slice for each guest, and his grace slid each slice onto a plate, where it was covered with a thin piece of parchment and carried by a footman to the recipient. The parchment was to hide any false cuts that would have been made in the kitchen if the knife had encountered the little treasure the cake held in its center and had to move across the obstacle. The revelation of the treasure, still referred to as the bean, was the high point of the evening. Harriet glanced at Julius, who was watching the proceedings rather idly, his fingers playing with a walnut shell on his plate.

The cake was finally distributed, and the twins held their breath, their fingers hovering over the parchment on their plates, their eyes on their grandfather, who would give the signal. Slowly, the Duke lifted his parchment clear, crumpling it in his hand beside his plate. Then he took up his fork and plunged it into the slice of cake.

Everyone followed suit. Harriet glanced at the children, watching with a smile as they threw aside the cake covering and drove their forks into the centers of their slices. "Oh!" Grace exclaimed first. "Look, Tom." She held up a cake-covered silver sovereign. "I found the bean."

"But so did I." Tom, sounding puzzled, lifted the sovereign's twin from his plate. "There are two beans in this cake. How did that happen?"

"How, indeed," murmured Harriet, glancing at her grandfather, who slowly dropped an eyelid in a conspiratorial wink. His indulgences were always surprises and all the more significant for that fact. It was unlikely the twins would both find favors in next year's Twelfth Night cake.

She turned to her own plate, carefully removing the parchment and taking a delicate forkful. "It's as delicious as ever," she said. "Mistress Hubbard has outdone herself again." She forked another piece.

"Harry, Harry, don't eat it!" Grace cried urgently. "You'll choke. There's something in it."

Harriet held up the fork and caught a glint of something among the raisins and candied fruit. She used her free hand to pry it loose. So this was how Julius had intended to make his announcement.

She wiped the ring on her napkin and held it up to the candlelight. It was exquisite. A thin gold circlet embedded with emeralds and seed pearls. As perfect and delicate as anything she could have imagined.

Julius took it from her and took her left hand. He held it for a moment, his dark eyes asking the question for the last time. Harriet nodded, and he slipped the ring onto her finger. Only then did she realize, as the table seemed to draw a collective breath, that forty pairs of eyes had been glued to this little play.

Julius stood up. "Ladies and gentlemen, I would like to announce that Lady Harriet has done me the great honor of agreeing to become my wife."

The table erupted in applause and clinking glasses, and above the din, the twins tugged at Harriet's arm. "Are you marrying the Earl, Harry?"

She looked into their solemn faces. "Yes, my dears, I am."

"But what will happen to us?"

"Only really good things," she said, drawing them tightly against her. "I promise you, only really good things will happen."

Grace took her face out of Harriet's bosom and

looked at Julius. "You'll be like a brother, won't you? Like Nick."

"Perhaps not just like Nick," he said gently. "But I will try to be what you need. I will look after you, love you, and care for you as Nick would have done. That much I can promise."

The Duke rose from his seat, lifting his glass. "A toast to a lifetime of happiness, my dears."

A lifetime of turbulence and excitement, Harriet thought, and she found the prospect utterly enticing. She sipped her wine, then raised her face for Julius's kiss. A kiss that embodied the promise of all that life could hold for them both.

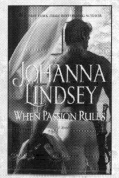
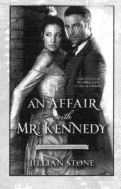

Fantasy.
Temptation.
Adventure.

Visit PocketAfterDark.com,
an all-new website just for Urban
Fantasy and Romance Readers!

- Exclusive access to the hottest
urban fantasy and romance titles!

- Read and share reviews on
the latest books!

- Live chats with your favorite
romance authors!

- Vote in online polls!

www.PocketAfterDark.com

26119

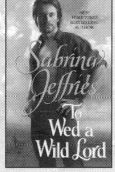

Printed in the United States
By Bookmasters